KITE
IDENTITY
BOOK TWO BAD COMPANY

HARRY EDGE

*Hodder
Children's
Books*

A division of Hachette Children's Books

A Catalogue record for this book is available
from the British Library

ISBN 978 0 340 99967 7

Typeset in Baskerville by Avon DataSet Ltd,
Bidford-on-Avon, Warwickshire

Printed in the UK by CPI Bookmarque Ltd, Croydon CR0 4TD

The paper and board used in this paperback by
Hodder Children's Books are natural recyclable products
made from wood grown in sustainable forests.
The manufacturing processes conform to the
environmental regulations of the country of origin.

Hodder Children's Books
A division of Hachette Children's Books
338 Euston Road, London NW1 3BH
An Hachette UK company
www.hachette.co.uk

For David, Sara Jane and Freya

Prologue

ISLINGTON, LONDON

The big house belonged to a government minister. Megan Kite's limo pulled up outside. Her bodyguard got out and scoped the street. Satisfied, he escorted the world's richest eighteen-year-old to the front door. She looked little like her photographs, but it was definitely her. Megan's hair had been dyed black. She was slim, tall and elegant. She wouldn't look so elegant soon.

Megan Kite dismissed the bodyguard. Good. That meant she would be easy to take. But not yet. Too many people arriving.

There were cheers from inside the house.

Surprise!

Balloons burst. The party began. Uh-oh. A police car drew up. No, it was OK, the police weren't going in. They were dropping off a scruffy youth. He wore jeans and a cheap T-shirt. His hair was tousled. He gave a nod of thanks to the driver, revealing his full face. Luke Kite. The heiress's younger brother. There was only one photo of him in circulation. Luke was more handsome in the flesh. Tall, with a furrowed brow. The sort of guy who took life a bit too seriously.

There was no reason to kidnap Luke. He didn't inherit the company. He had no power. Lucky for him. His big sister was about to have the worst birthday of her life.

One

It was only half past seven but the party was in full swing. The downstairs rooms were too rammed for conversation. Luke had just arrived and was looking for his sister. He had some big news for her but he needed to get her on her own.

The party wasn't Luke's idea of a good time. All of Megan's friends were older than him. They shouted a lot and acted real confident, though maybe that was the drink. There she was, in a pale cream dress. She had her arm round her boyfriend, Ethan. Luke charged over.

'Can I borrow Megan for a minute?'

'Sure.' Ethan had bounced into another conversation even before Luke could manoeuvre himself next to his sister.

'There's something I've got to tell you,' Megan shouted at Luke. 'Let's go somewhere quiet.'

'Fine. There's something I've got to tell you, too.'

'This way.'

Luke followed his sister down to the Thompsons' wine cellar.

'It's about the company,' Megan said.

'What are you going to do?' Luke asked. 'Sell it?'

'Kite Industries is too big and complicated to sell,' Megan

replied. 'And it's Dad's legacy. I want to make him proud of us.'

Luke didn't like it when Megan talked like Jack Kite was still alive. Their father was a hero to her. To Luke, he was the guy who knocked up his mom and signed the maintenance cheques. Luke had been closer to his uncle. For a while there, he'd thought that Mike Kite was his real father. Turned out he wasn't, which was what he was about to tell Megan. He'd just been given the results of his DNA test.

'We have to keep Kite Industries going,' Megan went on.

'What do you mean when you say *we*?' he asked Megan.

'I've been at my lawyer's. I signed over half of Kite Industries to you. You'll inherit when you're eighteen, like I just did.'

'That's . . .' Luke was flabbergasted. He had spent his entire life convincing himself that he wanted nothing to do with his dad's billions. '. . . mind blowing. Thank you.'

'We may only be cousins,' Megan said. 'but you're my whole family. And half of Dad's money is more than either of us could ever spend. I can't run Kite on my own. It's too big a responsibility. I need help.'

'You've got it,' Luke said. This was the moment when, on TV, the two would have hugged, but the Kites weren't big huggers. Thoughts shot through Luke's head. He was rich. He didn't have to go back to school. He didn't have to face all the gossip about his uncle and his mother, who were both in prison. He must phone his friend Andy, tell him. But first, he had to tell Megan about the DNA test. He realized that he was frowning with concentration and Megan was looking concerned.

'What was your news?' she asked.

Before Luke could answer, her boyfriend crashed down the stairs.

'*There* you are!' Ethan Thompson said. 'You've got a special delivery upstairs that you need to sign for in person.'

'I'll only be a minute,' Megan told Ethan. She was preoccupied, disappointed by Luke's reaction. She'd expected him to be more grateful. Or, at least, more excited.

'Oh.' Ethan realized he was interrupting something. 'I'll make him wait.'

'What was it you wanted to tell me?' Megan asked Luke.

'It'll take more than a minute.' Luke gave the funny, self-conscious smirk that always made Megan uncomfortable. 'Go get your package. I'll come with you.'

'OK.' Megan hurried up the stairs, followed by Luke. She waved at Ethan and his mum, then bumped into Flick. Flick was Megan's new personal assistant and probably her second-best friend.

'Who's this?' Flick asked.

'This is my cousin, Luke.'

'I've been so looking forward to meeting you!' Flick said.

Luke's eyes widened. Flick was a deadly blonde at the worst of times and tonight she was dressed to impress.

A bit of flirting might do Luke good, Megan thought. He was so wound up most of the time.

'You two ought to get to know each other,' Megan said. 'Excuse me.'

She pushed her way through the party to the front door. A guy in black leathers and a motorbike helmet waited patiently in the vestibule, holding a small, wrapped package.

'Megan Kite?'

'Yes.'

'Happy eighteenth birthday. Could you sign this, please?'

The guy held out a clipboard and what looked like a large pen. Only it wasn't a pen. Megan felt a dart pierce her chest. Then she fell forward. Somebody caught her.

That was the last thing she remembered for a long time.

Two

'How long have you known Megan?' Luke asked Flick. He was anxious to resume the conversation with his sister, but Flick was the prettiest girl he'd met on any of his visits to the UK. She was also the first person at this party keen to talk to him.

'Not long. I work for her. Kind of. We're friends, too.'

'You're the—'

'Personal assistant, yes!'

Luke remembered the phone conversation when Megan told him she'd hired someone to shop for her, travel with her and generally arrange her life. He'd been snarky about her having a kind of servant, but maybe it wasn't such a bad idea.

'You're thinking that this is an odd career choice,' Flick went on, 'but I'm not ready to go to university and I need to work. So I joined this agency who hooked me up with Megan. It's only been three weeks but we get on really well. She's always talking about you. She thinks of you as a kid brother. The way you interrupted her funeral! That's an amazing story.'

'I guess,' Luke said.

Luke didn't like to talk about the fake funeral. He had

interrupted it to stop an unlucky girl's body from being cremated in place of Megan. Shortly afterwards, his uncle was arrested. Somehow his father's murderer, Graham Palmer, managed to escape.

Luke's uncle, Mike Kite, had tried to make Dad's assassination look like an accident. He'd wanted Megan dead too, so that he would have control of the multi-billion-dollar Kite Industries. He claimed to have done everything for Luke. On the day of the funeral, Mike and Luke's mom, Crystal, had revealed to Luke that Mike was really his dad. Luke had been shattered by that news, but today, DNA tests – undertaken by Special Branch as part of their investigation into Mike – had proved that Jack Kite was Luke's father, no matter what Mom and Mike believed.

Luke didn't want to discuss any of this casually.

'Where do you live?' he asked Flick. 'Are you a London girl?'

'Born and bred. I think Ethan's trying to get your attention.'

Luke turned round. Ethan gestured with his hands to indicate 'phone' and pointed towards the landline in the corner of the room. Nobody used landlines any more. Why was somebody calling Luke here?

'Don't go away!' Luke told Flick.

'I won't.'

She must be at least nineteen, he thought. She couldn't be interested in a sixteen-year-old. Where was Megan? He picked up the phone.

'Hi. This is Luke Kite. Who is this?'

'My name is Celine Michel. Have you heard of me?'

'No. Should I have?'

'I was your father's girlfriend.'

'His . . . ?' Hearing the French accent, Luke made a connection. 'Did you leave a couple of messages on Dad's answering machine at the Barbican, just after he died?'

'Yes. That was me. I need to speak to you about Jack's death. There is something not right about the helicopter crash.'

'I agree,' Luke said. 'I expect you read how they arrested my uncle. Excuse me.'

Ethan was tapping him on the shoulder. 'Have you seen Megan?'

'Not for a few minutes. She went to the door, remember?' He returned to Celine. 'Why did you want to talk to me?'

'I need to speak to you in person,' Celine told him. 'In confidence. Can you come and see me in Nice?'

'In France? I suppose. It might be easier if you came here. We have a lot to figure out at the moment.'

'It is not safe for me to travel. I would be grateful if you could visit me very soon. I have important information about your father. I have a message I need to play to you.'

'What kind of message?'

'It was left by your father. You must hear it for yourself.'

This time the hand on his shoulder was Flick's. She pressed close to him. 'Luke, I think you'd better get off the phone. Nobody can find Megan anywhere.'

'Luke, are you still there?' the voice on the phone said.

'Uh, yeah. I'll just take down your contact info. Flick, have you got a pen? Celine, what's your number?'

She gave him her phone, email and postal address, but he

stopped writing after he'd taken the phone number. Behind him, he could hear the sound of rising panic. The word 'police' was mentioned. Flick looked agitated.

'I've got to go, Celine. I'll be in touch.'

He hung up.

Luke and Flick did a sweep of the party. No Megan. She wasn't outside, either. They found Ethan in the hall. He was explaining the situation to his mother. While he was talking, Ethan glanced at Luke, who shook his head.

'You're overdramatizing,' Florence Thompson told Ethan. 'We don't know that Megan's been kidnapped. She could have gone out for air or to buy something.'

'Leaving her own birthday party?' Ethan retorted.

'Have you tried ringing her mobile?'

'It goes straight to voicemail,' Luke told the government minister. 'I think we should phone the police.'

'That might be premature. Give her five more minutes.'

'She hasn't been seen for fifteen minutes,' Luke pointed out.

'A quarter of an hour is hardly—'

'It's my call,' Luke said. He had Ian Trevelyan on speed-dial. Ian was the senior Special Branch officer who had dealt with his father's murder. He would be on his way home from meeting Luke earlier in the day. That was when Ian had told him the DNA test results.

Ian answered at once. Luke explained the situation.

'She doesn't have a personal bodyguard?' Trevelyan asked.

'No.'

'And there's no security in the house?'

'I don't think so.'

10

'I'll get a car round there straight away. You ought to call Kite Industries, have them send a security team round too.'

Luke didn't have any of the UK Kite numbers on his phone. Until a few minutes ago, he'd had no remaining connection with the company. It took him a couple of minutes to track down the company's UK security desk. By the time he got through, a police car had pulled up outside. Ian Trevelyan got things done quickly.

Kite's new security chief was called Jim Pierce. Luke explained the seriousness of the situation to him.

'The police are here,' he finished. 'I'd better talk to them.'

'Hold on,' Jim said, in a rich Irish accent. 'We'll get to the bottom of this. I'm looking at the latest report from Ms Kite's security detail. She said Special Branch would be there.'

Megan must have meant Ian, who had chosen not to come. Ian had been asked as a friend, not in his official capacity, but Luke could understand the confusion.

'They weren't.'

'Put the police on the phone.'

Luke handed his mobile to a young sergeant. Then he looked down the street. Megan was bound to reappear at any moment. She'd have thought of something she needed from a store. Only there weren't any stores nearby. And she had a personal assistant who she could have sent. Why would anyone walk out of their own birthday party? He turned to Ethan.

'Did you see the package that arrived?'

Ethan shook his head. 'I got distracted.'

11

The sergeant returned Luke's phone. 'Are you Ms Kite's closest relative?' she asked.

'Yes, I'm her . . .' Luke didn't finish the sentence.

'We'll treat this very seriously. A senior Special Branch officer is on his way over. We've already put out an alert with a full description of your sister. Do you have a recent photo?'

'I've got some on my phone,' Ethan said.

Within moments, he was Bluetoothing the pictures to the officer's mobile, and the images were shooting around London.

Ian Trevelyan arrived, still wearing the powder-blue suit he'd had on in their earlier meeting. Luke summed up the situation for him. Florence Thompson added a few details.

'I'll never forgive myself if she was taken from here,' Mrs Thompson said.

Expensively-dressed students surrounded them. News of the police presence had filtered through to the partygoers.

'What's going on?' Grace asked. Ethan's sister still limped a little. She was recovering from a bad leg injury, sustained when a car ran her over in Scotland. It turned out that the driver, Graham Palmer, had mistaken her for Megan, who Mike had ordered him to kill.

Ethan told her what had happened. Grace yelled, 'Get the DJ to turn the music off!'

Megan's rich friends didn't know how to behave in these circumstances. The partygoers began to collect their coats. They seemed more excited than scared. The music stopped, leaving in its wake a babble of excited, nervous conversation.

Flick squeezed Luke's arm. 'This is dreadful,' she said. 'Is there anything I can do to help?'

'No, but thanks,' Luke said.

Ian Trevelyan's deep voice cut through the clamour.

'Nobody can leave until they've been interviewed by the police. Megan Kite has been missing for about twenty-five minutes. I'd like each of you to think about when you saw her last and whether you saw or heard anything suspicious.'

Two Kite security vehicles shot down the street. The police had parked discreetly, further up the road, but the Kite saloons parked right outside, blocking expensive vehicles into their Residents Only bays. A portly man in a black leather bomber jacket barged his way through the partygoers.

'Where's Luke Kite?'

Luke stepped forward.

'We need to get you out of here as quickly as possible.'

'I don't know about that,' Luke said.

'We may have more questions for Luke,' Trevelyan told Jim Pierce.

'If the British security services knew what they were doing, we wouldn't be in this situation,' Pierce said, reaching into an inner pocket of his jacket, revealing the body armour beneath. 'If you need to talk to Mr Kite, do it through me.'

He pulled out a business card and shoved it into Ian's hand. 'Let's go.'

'Wait!' Luke said. 'I want a word with Ian alone.'

A flicker of satisfaction crossed Trevelyan's face. Pierce looked like he was going to argue, then changed his mind.

'Quickly!' he said.

Luke ushered the Special Branch officer into the cloakroom, which, until a few minutes ago, had been full of partygoers' coats.

'I didn't get the chance to tell Megan what you told me,' he said. 'We were interrupted. The thing is, she told me that she's giving me half the company anyway. When that gets out, I may be the next target for whoever's taken her.'

'I'll keep that to myself,' Ian said. 'So should you.'

Luke joined Pierce. He didn't get the opportunity to speak to the Thompson family. Which didn't bother him. Megan's powerful friends had let her down. They were no use to him. Luke was on his own again.

Three

The party guests were gone and Ethan was in bits.

'Why did they drag Luke away?' Ethan asked his mum. 'Do they think he had something to do with this?'

'They probably did it to protect him,' his sister said. 'After all, we didn't do a very good job looking after Megan.'

'Luke's only Megan's cousin,' Ethan pointed out. 'He doesn't have any stake in Kite Industries.'

'Has Megan made a will?' Mum asked.

'I don't think so,' Ethan replied. It wasn't the sort of thing he'd ever discussed with Megan.

'Then Luke is her nearest relative and would inherit everything. That's reason enough to take him into some kind of protective custody.'

'You don't think he . . .'

Grace finished his sentence for him. 'Had something to do with this? No. Luke stood up for Megan. You saw how he was at the funeral.'

'I guess.' Ethan wasn't entirely convinced. Luke's father, Mike Kite, was a greedy, clever crook. His mother was a clueless bimbo. Megan insisted that she loved Luke like a brother and he admired that in her. But Ethan had to look out for his girlfriend, and that involved keeping a suspicious eye on Luke. Sure, Luke cared for Megan, but he was only her cousin, not her half-brother, as she used to believe. Caring had its limits. And there was a very big prize at stake: the second-biggest software company in the world. Tomorrow, Megan had a meeting scheduled to discuss the company and all its interests. Ethan told Mum and Grace what Megan had said about the meeting she had scheduled with the Kite Industries CEO.

'You don't think the prospect of owning the whole company was too much for her,' Mum said. 'That she . . . ?'

'Did a runner?' Grace filled in. 'No way.'

Ethan stared out of the window. The street was festooned with yellow-and-black police tape. The last few days, Megan had been preoccupied. She said it was the prospect of taking over the company. Ethan worried she was going to dump him. He was starting university and she was about to be very busy. They'd not committed to each other. Far from it. When they talked about the future, they'd agreed not to rush things.

Ethan wanted to travel, to do good work where the fancy took him. Not to be tied down. He'd never been with a girlfriend for more than three months. That was how long he'd been seeing Megan. He was her first serious boyfriend. How serious was Ethan? For years, he'd regarded Megan as his kid sister's rich best friend, her near lookalike buddy. He'd kissed her once, when she was fifteen. Then he'd backed off. This year, she'd grown up and found herself in all sorts of danger. Ethan was drawn to danger. He'd flown halfway round the world to help her. Logic said she should be the one to fall heavily, not him.

But he had.

KITE INDUSTRIES HQ, LONDON

Luke was squashed between two heavily built goons on the back seat of an armoured saloon. Pierce spent most of the journey using his BlackBerry. Luke brooded about what to do.

'I want to see whoever's in charge,' Luke said, when they arrived in Soho.

'Stella Lock's in the air, so I can't reach her for instructions,' Pierce said. Lock was the company's acting chief executive. 'You'd better come to my office.'

Grumpy jerk. Luke reminded himself that Pierce's predecessor had been killed while trying to protect Megan. The security chief had every reason to think that Luke was trouble. Best, Luke thought, to hold back and play this cautiously.

'What does your intelligence say?' Luke asked Jim Pierce when they were alone. Pierce put down his BlackBerry.

'Not much, so far. I'm getting CCTV images from the area. We're liaising with Scotland Yard. And I've got somebody looking into groups and individuals with a motive for attacking our company, and Megan in particular.'

'Number one on the list being Mike Kite?'

'Yes. Your father is in custody, but that doesn't mean he can't get instructions out. We think we eliminated those people loyal to him within KI, but you can never be sure.'

'What motive would Mike have for kidnapping Megan?'

'She could be a bargaining chip. But our prime suspect

must be the assassin your father used, Graham Palmer. Palmer no longer has an employer, but he does have a grudge against Megan, and against you.'

'When was he last heard of?'

'Palmer disappeared off the face of the earth the day your father was arrested.'

Luke didn't like the way Pierce pointedly kept referring to Mike as 'your father', but he held his tongue. He hadn't had the chance to tell Megan about the DNA test, so he certainly wasn't going to tell Pierce.

'Do you know anything about a woman called Celine Michel?' Luke asked the security chief.

Pierce pressed a few keys on his computer. Luke would have liked to know what information was on there.

'She was your father's girlfriend. He was seeing her for about six months before his death. She lives in Nice, France. Why do you ask?'

'I was on the phone with her when Megan was taken.'

'You think she was trying to distract you?'

'I don't know.'

'Do you know if Megan made a will?'

'No, I don't. We didn't have those kind of conversations.'

This wasn't true, Luke realized as soon as he'd said it. The conversation about KI ownership was exactly that kind of conversation. The phone rang. Pierce listened for a couple of minutes before speaking again.

'Nothing very relevant on CCTV so far. There appears to have been a motorcyclist waiting outside the Thompson house for a good half hour before Megan was taken. I'm going to liaise with the police now, see if they can track them down. You just flew in. You probably need some rest. Where are you staying?'

Luke had been invited to stay at the Thompson house, but that no longer seemed such a good idea.

'My father's . . . I mean Jack Kite's old Barbican flat, I guess.'

'Fine. The security there was upgraded only last week. I'll have a helicopter take you from our roof.'

'I'm uncomfortable with 'copters. I've not been in one since . . .'

'Get used to it. This is London. Half of our roads are gridlocked. You either take the tube or a helicopter, and you're too vulnerable to use public transport.'

Graham Palmer had shot down Luke's father's helicopter using a long-range missile and a tracking system that Jack Kite had himself designed. If Palmer could get his dad that way, over the North Sea, Luke's enemies could easily get him over London, where there were a million places to hide a weapon.

But Luke didn't want to lose face and he knew he had to conquer his fear. He took the elevator to the roof.

Four

THE BARBICAN, LONDON

Luke let himself in to the Barbican apartment and smelled perfume. He didn't know the names of perfumes, but he recognized this smell from earlier in the day. It was classier than the stuff his mom wore, less sweet. A voice called out.

'Megan?'

'No, it's Luke.' He opened the door to the living area.

'Luke!' Flick got up from the chaise longue, the slit in her black leather skirt revealing a well-shaped thigh. 'I thought you were staying at the Thompsons'.'

'This is my place too. I hardly know the Thompsons.'

'Is there any news on Megan?'

'No. I was hoping you were her.'

'Sorry. Megan gave me a passcode and told me to use the spare room whenever I wanted. I have . . . issues with my parents, but I can't afford a place of my own. I'll get going.'

'No. Stay. Please. I could do with some company.'

He told her what had happened since they last met. It took a while. Flick listened attentively, asking intelligent questions, smiling sympathetically when he needed her to.

'Have you eaten?' she asked when he was done.

'Not since breakfast.'

'Let me fix you something.'

Luke took a shower. He felt wrung out.

In the kitchen, Flick had fixed him a tuna sandwich.

'I'd better go home,' she said, after they had talked about Megan some more. 'We don't really know each other well enough for me to stay the night in the same flat as you.'

Luke wanted to get to know her. 'I understand,' he said.

'We could meet up tomorrow,' Flick offered. 'Megan wanted me to help you out. She said the two of us ought to take you shopping for clothes.'

'Clothes?'

'She reckoned you need some new stuff.'

Luke wasn't interested in fashion, but he'd only brought enough clothes to last him for three days.

'It might keep me busy, I suppose.'

They exchanged numbers but Luke didn't commit to the idea. He would go if nothing important came up, if he needed distracting.

Flick had a KI credit card, she told him. Money wasn't a problem. Saying goodbye, she kissed him on the cheek.

'Try not to worry too much,' she said. 'Megan's tough. Whatever's happening to her, she'll get through it.'

ISLINGTON, LONDON

Grace slept badly, worried sick about her best friend. She felt terrible that Megan had been kidnapped from her home, where she should have been safe. What made things even worse was that, recently, their friendship had felt threatened – first, by Megan going out with her brother; second, by the arrival of Flick.

Grace had to make amends. So, over a late breakfast, she had a go at her mother.

'You're a government minister! You must know something.'

'There's been no ransom demand yet,' Mum replied. 'Megan can't officially be a missing person until she's been gone twenty-four hours. It's only been . . .' Mum looked at her watch. It was just after ten. 'Fifteen.'

'I'm going to look through Megan's room,' Grace said. 'See if there's anything the police missed that might give us a clue.'

'I'll come with you,' Ethan said.

Although Megan had a flat of her own, in the Barbican, lately she'd spent most of her time at the Thompson house. The biggest guest room was permanently set aside for her. Ethan followed his sister up to that room.

'She'll be OK,' he said, trying to be comforting.

'You can't *know* that!' Grace snapped.

He shut up and they started on the room. It felt odd, going through Megan's things.

'I don't know what we're looking for,' Grace said. 'There's her old mobile here. Think we should check that?'

She turned the phone on. Immediately, it began to ring.

'If you don't answer it,' Ethan said, 'I will.'

Grace pressed *receive*. 'Hello?'

'Megan, this is Celine Michel. Do you know who I am?'

22

'This isn't Megan. This is her friend, Grace. Can I ask why you're calling?'

'It's a personal matter. Is Megan there?'

'No. She's . . . indisposed.'

The French voice sounded exasperated.

'Is Luke staying with you? I don't have his mobile number.'

'I think he's staying in the Barbican flat. I don't have his mobile number either, I'm afraid. Can I give a message to Megan?'

'Please ask her to call me. Tell her it's about her father.'

'I will, but . . . she may be a while.'

'Who was that?' Ethan asked, when Grace had hung up.

'I have no idea.'

THE BARBICAN, LONDON

Luke woke early obsessing over what had happened to Megan. At six, he gave up trying to get back to sleep and turned on the TV news. There was nothing about Megan.

At nine, the phone rang. Luke hurried to answer it. The French woman from yesterday. Celine Michel. Luke apologized for not having called her back.

'Something came up,' he said. 'What was it that you wanted to discuss with me?'

'It is important I tell you in person. Please come to Nice.'

Luke wanted to keep her talking. 'Can you at least give me a clue?'

'It is about your father. I have things to show you.

Telling you would not be enough and it is not safe for me to leave Nice.'

'Really?' What she wanted to say might be connected to what had happened to Megan. Luke had to take this very seriously. 'I might be able to fly to Nice. I'll check the flights, get back to you later.'

He needed to get a KI credit card, Luke realized. It was crazy that Megan's personal assistant had one, while he didn't.

'OK,' Celine said, disappointment in her voice. She wanted him to commit to coming straight away. But Luke needed to check her out further. Should he trust her? It was an awful big coincidence that she had phoned him just as Megan was being kidnapped yesterday.

'I look forward to meeting you,' he said.

'And me you. Your father talked about you a great deal.'

'Did he?' Luke found this hard to believe. He and Jack Kite were never close. But Celine was only being polite, he told himself. There was no need to give her a hard time.

'Yes. He worried about you and your future. Please telephone me as soon as you know when you can come.'

Luke rang Ian Trevelyan. He told the Special Branch man about the conversation and his suspicions about Celine.

'Do you think I should go to Nice?' he asked.

'No. It could be a trap. Let me check her out and get back to you.'

'Is there any news on Megan?'

'Not yet. You'll be the first to hear, I promise.'

'There's nothing about her on the TV news.'

'That's because, last night, KI took out an injunction to stop publication. They say publicity might harm Megan's chances.'

'Or the stock price. I plan to see Stella Lock today.'

'Ask her to call me. She's been ducking my calls.'

Luke had yet to meet KI's acting Chief Executive Officer. If necessary, he decided, he would tell her about how Megan had signed over half the company to him. Which meant that, in the long term, he was Stella's boss. He called Kite Industries HQ and asked to speak to her.

'Ms Lock's not in yet,' her secretary said. 'Can I ask what this is regarding?'

'She'll know what it's about. Have her call me when she gets in, please,' Luke said. Then he rang Flick.

'I've been awake for hours and there's nothing I can do at the moment. Still want to take me shopping?'

'Love to. There's a store called Billionaire on Sloane Street in Knightsbridge,' she told him. 'Let's meet there.'

Luke rang Ethan to see if he'd heard anything. He hadn't.

'Hang tough,' he told Luke.

Luke told Ethan where he would be, then took the elevator. Dad once told him that four thousand people lived on the Barbican estate, but it always seemed eerily quiet to Luke. He met nobody on the way down.

Outside, he turned the wrong way, past Shakespeare Tower, with its police station at the bottom, towards the Barbican Centre, where Dad once took him to see some Cuban musicians. In front of the building were café tables, a large artificial lake, some palm trees. It might be a good place to hang out, but not in October. Opposite was the girls' school that Megan had attended before transferring to Brunts in Scotland.

Having got his bearings, Luke turned back. There was no room for cars in the Barbican complex, so no taxis to summon. A sign pointed him towards the tube station. It'd have to do. Climbing the concrete steps that took him that way, Luke decided that he didn't like these buildings. Dad used to argue that the concrete blocks were a modern architectural masterpiece. 'Brutalist' he called them. Sure, there was something brutal about them, but Luke thought 'boring' a better description.

Luke retraced his steps to Shakespeare Tower. That was when he noticed that he was being followed by two men. One was white, stocky. The other was Middle Eastern, more wiry, with black, curly hair. Maybe they weren't following Luke. Maybe they were just heading in the same direction as him. But Luke had long since learned that it paid to be paranoid.

Luke stopped by the Shakespeare Tower police station which, he saw now, was closed.

The men stopped too.

Were they the same people who had taken Megan?

Luke stepped up his pace. He sped up one set of steps, then another. Instead of heading for the tube station, he made for the Barbican Estates Office. He passed a small park, a children's playground. He could tell at a glance that the office was closed. He looked behind him, in time to see the Middle Eastern man pointing in his direction. There was no doubting it now. The men were following him. He had to lose them.

To his right, he could see a way out of the complex. He could also see one of the Barbican's uniformed security guards. The guy was about to enter the nearest tower block.

'Excuse me!' Luke called to him, then hurried to the door.

He was out of sight of the men, at least for a few moments.

'Yeah?'

Luke could ask for protection, but that was over the top. His situation was hard to prove and, anyway, he wanted to meet Flick, not go into hiding.

'There are two guys behaving very suspiciously, heading in this direction.' Luke described them.

'What do you mean, *suspiciously*?'

Easiest, Luke decided, to lie. 'Look, I'm in a hurry, but there's a young girl on her own, about ten, just over there.' He pointed towards the empty park. 'I think they're following her.'

'All right, thanks.' The security guard shot off in the direction that Luke had pointed. Luke hurried out on to the Aldersgate Road, which, thankfully, was quiet. He ran across it to the Barbican tube station. A blackboard had been tied to the railings.

Station Closed.

Five

The room was dark. Megan tried to remember where she was. Her eyes should be used to the darkness by now, but she could see nothing. No, wait. There was something covering her eyes. A sleep mask? Megan went to take it off. That was when she realized that her hands were tied.

She mustn't panic, Megan told herself. There had to be an explanation for what was happening. She was hot and sweaty. Her head felt heavy, like she had a hangover, or worse. Maybe she was still asleep. Were she and Ethan out somewhere last night? Of course, it was her eighteenth party. Now Megan got it. Her friends had played a joke on her. They'd spiked her drink. Not a very funny joke.

No. This wasn't a dream. Megan wasn't sure how long she'd been asleep, but she was awake now, and badly needed to pee. Her mouth was incredibly dry, and she needed a drink, too. She opened her mouth to call out. That was when she realized she'd been gagged.

THE BARBICAN, LONDON

There were 'renovation works' taking place on the District Line and Hammersmith and City lines. Arrows pointed in the direction of the nearest two tube stations, both five minutes' walk away. Luke looked behind him. No sign of the men. No sign of a taxi on the wide road, either. It was a Saturday and this was a business district, so there was hardly anybody about.

He could run down a side road, lose them that way. But London wasn't like Brooklyn, or New York, where most streets were laid out on a grid that was easy to understand. Luke would quickly get lost. And there were two of them, both of whom were likely to know the area better than he did.

Luke cursed himself for not having satnav on his phone. He decided to run down Aldersgate Road, towards St Paul's. He would flag down a cab on the way or, failing that, get to the tube station next to St Paul's Cathedral.

The road was wide, but not too long. At the bottom of it was a circular-shaped building. Once he rounded the building, Luke would be impossible to catch. He hoped.

The round building stood in front of the last remaining section of a wall that the Romans had built around London. Good at locking people in, the Romans. And keeping the riff-raff out. Luke wondered what the Romans would have done to America, if they'd ever made it there. He heard traffic and looked back, hoping for a taxi. Instead, he saw his two pursuers. They had seen him, and were running in his direction.

Luke hurried across the road, dodging traffic. What to do? He could try to outrun the men, and make it to St Paul's tube. He was already halfway there. Or he could turn left along London Wall Road.

Or . . . the rotunda, he now saw, was the entrance to the Museum of London. It occupied the middle of the road junction as though it were an enormous roundabout. In front of Luke was a glass-fronted alcove containing an escalator, with a sign pointing towards the museum entrance.

Luke made up his mind. He jumped on to the escalator then ran up it, hoping that his pursuers wouldn't be able to work out where he had gone. He got to the top, then took the walkway that ran above the rotunda, which had a garden below. Even if the men found him, there would be people here. There would be places for Luke to hide, or seek protection.

He kept his head down and ran along the walkway. The museum was free. No queue to get in. He turned right to the exhibits. On his left were hoardings, behind which new displays were being set up. To his right were a series of rooms containing historical displays.

Luke looked behind him. No sign of the two men. How long ought he to hang out here before he went to meet Flick? Fifteen, twenty minutes? He walked from room to room, passing timelines showing the development of the city. He wandered through areas showcasing the theatre and a War, Plague and Fire display. He ought to be interested in this stuff, of course, but he wasn't, even at the best of times. Still no sign of the men. Had he lost them? Should they turn up, there were plenty of people around. They wouldn't find it easy to take him.

Perhaps he ought to call Ian. And Flick, to let her know that he'd be late. He got out his phone. Poor signal.

Luke completed the circuit of the building. He was about to enter Reception when he noticed the Middle Eastern man from before. He was showing an attendant a photograph, presumably of Luke. His sidekick, the stocky man, was standing by the only exit door. Luke squeezed behind a hoarding about the new Modern London display. He was trapped.

ISLINGTON, LONDON

Grace had to talk to somebody about what was going on. Ethan had been on his computer since they searched Megan's room. Mum had gone to the Home Office. Dad was in Brussels. She decided to ring Luke. His phone went straight to answering service without once ringing.

'Who are you calling?' It was her brother.

'Luke. I wanted to see if he'd found out anything.'

'He rang me half an hour ago. Said he was meeting Flick in Knightsbridge to buy some clothes.'

'Megan's been kidnapped and Luke's out *shopping*? What kind of cousin is he?'

'He's probably fallen under Flick's spell, the way Megan did,' Ethan said. 'Or maybe he just needs clean clothes.'

'Flick's such a bimbo and such a flirt. I never understood why Megan hired her,' Grace said.

'They get on well. We don't need all our friends to be super-bright, do we?'

'Flick's not Megan's friend,' Grace pointed out. 'She's an employee.'

'Sure, and Luke's a sixteen-year-old. He's probably never had a girl as hot as Flick look at him before. Anyway, he's too young to be much help in finding Megan.'

'I suppose you're right.' Grace didn't like it when her elder brother condescended to her. She'd liked it even less when, by getting off with Megan, Ethan had stolen her best friend. But now the two of them were equally affected by Megan's kidnapping. It ought to bring them closer together.

'What are we going to do?' she asked her big brother.

'All we can do is wait.'

Six

THE MUSEUM OF LONDON

The Middle Eastern man had gone into the museum displays, looking for Luke. His sidekick still guarded the only exit.

Luke checked his phone again. At the front of the building there was one bar of signal. He might be able to make a call, but who to? The Middle Eastern man wouldn't be long. While the new displays were being set up, this place was pretty small, as museums went. His pursuer could check out all of the open rooms within five minutes. Then he was bound to find Luke.

Was there another way out? Luke could go back into the exhibit space, but then the stocky sidekick at the door would spot him. He could go to the information desk, ask for help, but the woman behind the desk didn't look like she could stand up to the gorilla waiting by the exit.

Luke was behind a three-metre-high billboard about a forthcoming exhibition. He couldn't be seen from the front door, but he could be seen by anyone who was leaving the exhibition and happened to glance in his direction.

A group of Scandinavian tourists were coming out of the

museum shop opposite him. They all wore orange baseball caps, to help their guide identify them. The guide was trying to get the group together so that they could leave. One of the group dawdled only a few feet away from Luke. He was about Luke's size and only a couple of years older. He wore a thin, grey fleece. Luke beckoned him over. The youth gave Luke a suspicious look, but came.

'Yes?'

'I really like your baseball cap. Would you sell it to me?'

'Sell?'

Luke had a better idea. 'I'll tell you what, if you agree to help me, how about an exchange . . .'

The tour guide had the whole group together. She called to Luke's new friend, who waved in acknowledgment. He and Luke agreed their deal. Luke took off his leather jacket and handed it to the Swede. He put on the orange baseball cap. Head down, he joined the tour group.

At the exit, the stocky blond man stood aside to let the group pass. Luke got by him. He glanced back to see the man giving close attention to the Swede in the leather jacket. He could tell that it wasn't Luke, though, and he hadn't come close enough before to be sure that it was the same leather jacket.

Luke stayed with the tour group all the way to the escalator. Once on it, they were out of view. Luke breathed a huge sigh of relief.

'Hey, you!'

It was the tour guide.

'You are not with us.'

'No, I . . .'

34

'It's OK,' said the youth in Luke's leather jacket, adding something in Swedish or Danish or wherever he was from. Then he slapped Luke on the back.

'I think you need your coat back. It is cold out here.'

Luke smiled.

'You only needed to ask. I would have helped you anyway.'

'Thanks.'

At the bottom of the escalator, Luke returned the cap, put on his jacket, then ran like the blazes, following a sign that pointed towards St Paul's tube station. He hoped it wasn't far.

It wasn't. In New York, important buildings usually had space around them so that people could appreciate and admire them. Not in chaotic London. Here, the top of the famous cathedral jutted above a mess of buildings that tightly surrounded it. Amongst them was the entrance to a tube station. Luke ran across the road and descended the subway. He had just enough British coins to buy a ticket that would take him across London.

In the station lobby he read the underground map and worked out that he would need to change lines once to get to Knightsbridge. He got on to the Central line, where a sign informed him that there would be a train in two minutes.

Twenty minutes later, he was in Knightsbridge, looking for the store where he was to meet Flick.

Megan's personal assistant was waiting outside a chic, black-fronted store. She wore a white, belted trench coat.

Black stockinged legs. Her heels made her nearly as tall as Luke.

'I'd almost given up on you,' she said.

Luke explained what had happened.

'That's terrible. Shouldn't you go to the police? Or the Kite people?'

'I'm going there soon anyway,' Luke said. 'The last thing I want is to be tied up with the police until then. I'll tell Jim Pierce about it when I go in to see Stella Lock.'

Flick looked dubious. 'We'd better get on with it then.'

They avoided the most famous stores, Harrods and Harvey Nichols, in favour of smaller but even more expensive places. Luke didn't like shopping for clothes and today it was especially hard to concentrate. He kept looking at Flick rather than the shirts and stuff that she picked out. At Prada, he let her buy him some Italian shoes.

'Have you ever been to Italy?' Luke asked Flick.

'Of course. Haven't you?'

'I've hardly been anywhere.'

'I thought your dad took you all over the world.'

'He took Megan, not me.'

In the end, Luke settled on some Superdry jeans and Boss T-shirts, together with a DKNY jacket. They were only better designed versions of the simple gear he wore at home, but they were what he felt comfortable in. Flick, to her credit, didn't try to get him to choose anything more complicated or chic. He liked being with her. He wished that she was a couple of years younger. Then she might see him as a potential boyfriend.

'Have you noticed those guys?' she asked. 'I think they might be following us around.'

Luke glanced back. Too late. It was the men from before. They began to run towards them. Luke swore.

'We're in danger,' he told Flick.

'We can't be in danger, we're in Knightsbridge!'

The men reached Luke and Flick. They each grabbed one of his arms.

'You have to come with us!' the Middle Eastern one said.

The two men lifted Luke off his feet and began to hurry him down the busy Sloane Street, pushing shoppers out of the way. Luke cast an anxious look back at Flick. She was stood in the middle of the pavement, surrounded by shopping bags.

The men stopped by a black Mercedes. They pushed Luke on to the back seat.

'What's going on?' Luke asked. 'Where are we going?'

'Kite HQ,' the white one said.

Those were the only words that either man spoke on the way to Soho.

'Are you taking me to see Stella Lock?' Luke asked as the men dragged him into the building.

'Hardly,' the white one said.

A minute later, he found himself back in Jim Pierce's office. The burly Irishman folded his arms and leaned forward.

'Nice shopping trip?' Jim Pierce asked Luke.

'I needed clothes,' Luke replied, responding to the sarcasm in the question.

'Glad you weren't too busy worrying about your sister.'

'Why were you having those guys follow me? Why didn't

you just phone me, ask me to come in?'

'Because I doubted that you would.' Pierce gave Luke a hard, long look. 'You weren't entirely honest with me yesterday.'

'What do you mean?'

'You said you knew nothing about your sister's will.'

'I don't. All I know is what she told me about dividing up the ownership of KI.'

'So you don't deny that she told you about that? Good.'

'What do you mean, "don't deny"?' Luke asked. 'It was a surprise when she told me. I was only just starting to take it in yesterday, when she vanished, which is why I didn't mention it.'

Pierce's frown hardened. 'The new agreement, a copy of which was hand-delivered to Ms Lock this morning, doesn't come into full effect until your eighteenth birthday, which is twenty months away. The agreement makes it clear that, until then, your role is an advisory and development one, with all decisions to be deferred to your sister and the KI board. In other words—'

'I have no power here whatsoever. I get it. But I still want to meet Stella Lock and to find out who the prime suspects are in my sister's kidnapping.'

'Funny you should mention that. I'm about to subject the prime suspect to an intense interrogation. Here's the dossier.'

The file that Pierce handed to Luke consisted of three sheets of paper listing organizations and individuals, any one of which might have a motive for attacking KI in general or Megan in particular. They ranged from terrorist groups to businessmen and women, hardly any of whom he'd heard of.

There were so many people on the list that Luke found it hard to take in. How could KI have made so many enemies?

'Is this serious?' Luke asked. 'Can there really be this many people who'd even consider kidnapping my sister? This list doesn't seem to be prioritized in any way.'

'Oh, but it is,' Jim Pierce said. 'If you look at the last page, you'll see that there's only one person with a strong motive and opportunity.'

Luke turned the page. There were only four words on it.

Prime suspect was the heading. Beneath that, it read:

Luke Kite.

Seven

ISLINGTON, LONDON

Luke's mobile was now switched off, not even taking messages.

'There must be something we can do,' Ethan said to Grace.

Grace could see the fire in his eyes. Her brother wasn't the sort of person who backed away from a fight. He had once flown halfway round the world to help Megan, and that was before he was going out with her. Her brother slumped on to the living room's wide leather sofa.

The room exploded.

There was broken glass everywhere. Grace ran to the window but the motorbike they could hear was already disappearing into the distance. At least it wasn't a bomb, only a brick. Ethan picked up the phone. Grace picked up the red brick. There was a note attached to it with a piece of string. Before looking at it, Grace had to shake the broken glass from her hair.

Grace opened the envelope and blood dripped on to the message. A shard of glass had pierced her cheek.

To Home Office Minister Florence Thompson.

We have Megan Kite. She will only be released when Kite Industries has completely withdrawn its workers from Burma and severed all contact with Burma's military dictatorship. We undertake this action with reluctance. Megan Kite <u>was warned</u>, but chose to ignore our warning. Now her life is set against the freedom of millions. Tell Kite to withdraw at once.

BMFF

Burma? What did Kite Industries or Megan have to do with Burma? Grace wasn't even sure if the country was in Asia or Africa. Was Burma even *called* Burma any more? The whole thing was ridiculous. And what did that mean: *Megan Kite <u>was warned</u>*?

KITE INDUSTRIES HQ, LONDON

This was the fifth hour of questioning. If Megan was dead, which Luke didn't like to think about, he effectively owned KI. But its head of security was still treating him like a criminal.

'You knew that Megan hadn't made a will and you – being legally her brother, regardless of who your father is – were her closest relative. As soon as she turned eighteen and inherited the company, you had her taken,' Pierce accused.

'I must have moved quickly,' Luke snarled. 'Megan only told me about the will two minutes before she was kidnapped.'

'So you claim. The evidence points the other way.'

'Bring it on,' Luke said. 'But this is a load of bull.'

'No need for us to deal with you,' Pierce replied. 'We'll probably just send you home. Sixteen-year-olds are treated rather more harshly over there than they are here, aren't they?'

Luke had had enough. 'I have a British passport,' he pointed out. 'When are you going to hand me over to the British police? They have the right to question me. You don't.'

'Don't talk to me about rights,' Pierce told him. 'What rights did Megan have when you had her snatched from her eighteenth birthday party yesterday?'

'I've had it with you!' Luke said. 'I'm going.'

'No.'

'Then get me a lawyer.'

Pierce laughed. He was still laughing when the door opened. Sayeed came in. He was the Middle Eastern man who had followed Luke earlier. Sayeed leaned over Pierce and whispered in his ear. The smile faded from the security chief's face.

'Keep an eye on him,' Pierce told Sayeed, then left the room.

Luke looked at the bodyguard.

'Have they found her?' he asked

Sayeed gave the smallest shake of the head. Pierce returned.

'You're free to go,' he told Luke. 'I'm sorry that we held you for so long and that I questioned you so hard, but your father was responsible for the murder of our founder and there was a real fear that you had done the same to his daughter. I'm sure that, in time, you'll see that my actions were justified.'

Luke held his tongue. He didn't want to do anything rash.

'Sayeed, I'd like you and Carl to take Mr Kite home, please. Stay with him and I'll set up a bodyguard detail to replace you. By the way, Luke, Ian Trevelyan would like you to call him.'

'OK,' Luke said, but he was too angry to talk to anyone. Only when he was in the helicopter, waiting for the pilot, did Luke get out his mobile and make the call.

'What happened, Ian? I had Jim Pierce giving me the third degree for hours. Then he suddenly changed his tune, told me to go home.'

'They've had a ransom demand. It seems the group who've got Megan are Burmese freedom fighters.'

'Burma? What's Kite Industries got to do with Burma?'

'I'd like to find that out, too. I'm trying to arrange a meeting with Kite Industries' acting CEO, a woman called Stella Lock.'

'Do you think this ransom demand's real, that these Burmese freedom fighters really have Megan?'

'They haven't offered any proof yet, so we can't be sure. The good news is that, if they're pro-democracy activists, they're far less likely to harm Megan, no matter what happens.'

He was starting to get used to travelling on a helicopter. Beneath Luke, the city went about its business, a gigantic game board featuring figures tinier than ants, with roads filled by endless coloured counters. From this height, it was easy to think of people as tokens in a game. Even his sister.

Eight

Hour after hour passed. Megan tried to figure out who had done this to her. Uncle Mike was the most obvious suspect. But Mike was in a maximum security prison in the USA, barred from all communication with anyone but his lawyers and close family. He shouldn't be in a position to cause mischief.

Megan kept thinking about the timing of her kidnap. Yesterday (or, given her fuzziness over time, the day before) was the day she inherited. Today she was meant to meet the acting CEO of KI, Stella Lock, to discuss how she was going to run the business. She'd been planning to take Luke to the meeting too, work out a role for him, even if he couldn't, technically, become a director until he, too, turned eighteen. Did someone want her out of the way before that meeting?

Megan's mouth was dry. She had a crushing headache. If the blindfold weren't there, she would cry her eyes out. When would someone come? Megan tried to think who had a motive to hurt her. She dreaded the thought that Luke might be behind it. Her cousin could have arranged the kidnap before he knew that she was signing over half the company to him. Only why would he? They had issues, of course they did, but Luke had proved his loyalty to her more than once. No, it couldn't be him.

Who else did that leave? Some ex-girlfriend of Ethan's, maybe. There were plenty of them, though nobody serious. At least that was what he'd said. He also said that one of them took it pretty hard when he said they had no future.

But Ethan wouldn't date a psycho. No, it had to be to do with Kite Industries. Megan went over every conversation she'd had, every briefing she'd read. KI, she'd discovered since her dad's death, was a huge, multinational conglomerate. The firm's operations were not exclusively devoted to computer software, although software remained its biggest focus. Dad and Mike had diversified, spreading funds into all sorts of other areas. Some of these were only loosely linked with the software side: aviation, for instance, and communication systems for high-velocity weapons. Not something she was entirely comfortable with, but give it time. Once she'd got her feet under the desk, and the Chief Executive reported to her, Megan would make some changes. At least, that was the plan before this happened.

Her arms ached. Her legs ached. She wanted to cough and she could barely breathe. What if her nose got blocked? She could suffocate to death. She tried to figure out who knew where she was. Her relationship with Ethan wasn't widely known. Nor was the location of her party, which had only been given out at the last minute. Her friends had been told to keep the evening free, but they would have expected the event to be at a club. In fact, a club had been booked for later, with a live set from . . . what was that?

Megan heard a key turning in a lock.

THE BARBICAN, LONDON

Sayeed and his sidekick followed Luke out of the helicopter.

'You can leave!' he shouted at them, over the engine noise. 'I don't need you here.'

'Those aren't our instructions,' Sayeed said.

'I don't care. You work for Jim Pierce, not for me, and you virtually kidnapped me this morning. Nobody else is chasing me. So leave me alone!'

Reluctantly, the two men got back into the 'copter. Luke waited until he was sure they were gone, then strode across the forecourt to BS Johnson Tower. He turned on his mobile. Missed calls and texts from Flick, Ethan, Grace and Ian Trevelyan.

Flick was waiting for Luke in the apartment. She hugged him and he told her what had happened. Then he rang Grace to found out what was in the ransom note. Nothing that Jim Pierce hadn't already told him.

'Did Megan ever say anything to you about Burma?' Luke asked.

'Not that I can remember.'

'I think we should see what we can find out.'

He and Flick used the net to research Burma. The country was run by a military dictatorship who preferred to call the country Myanmar. They had kept the democratically elected leader under house arrest for years and years. Stuff like that didn't tend to appear on US TV networks, so it was all news to Luke. The freedom fighters, it seemed, were in the right. Which didn't explain why Kite Industries was being targeted by them.

'Question is,' Luke said, 'what's KI up to in Burma?'

The landline rang. Luke hadn't returned any of the calls from earlier. He expected it to be Grace, or Ian. But it was Celine Michel. For the third time, he put her off.

Nine

'I'm sorry we had to leave you for so long,' the voice said. 'We had security issues.'

The voice was calm, almost caring. The accent was foreign, but gave no clue as to the speaker's first language.

'I'm going to walk you through to the bathroom. I'll untie you so that you can clean up. Then we will be able to talk. OK?'

Megan nodded. She felt rank.

'Walk slowly.' The woman took Megan's arm. 'Let me guide you. There are some steps coming up.'

Megan stumbled. After who-knew-how-many hours tied up, her body was full of shooting cramp pains. One of her feet had gone to sleep. The woman with the gentle voice held on to her, kept her upright. They walked several more paces, then stopped. Megan heard a door open, smelled antiseptic.

'In a moment, I'm going to untie you. But first I must warn you. Do not try to run. You are a long way from home and there are many of us here to stop you. We do not want to hurt you but will do whatever is necessary to prevent you from escaping. Do not remove your blindfold until I have closed the door behind you. That is for your safety as much as mine. You will be given twenty minutes, after which I will knock on the door. You must put the blindfold back on before opening the door. Understood?'

Megan nodded.

'OK, I'm going to take off your gag now. Please do not try to shout. There is nobody but us within hearing distance.'

She undid the gag. Megan sucked in air. Her throat felt brittle and she began to cough.

'D-drink?' she said, when the coughing fit was over.

'Here.' A plastic bottle was put in her hand. Megan swigged from it. 'There are fresh clothes for you. Leave your old ones on the floor. OK?'

'OK,' Megan said. 'But I need to know. Who are you? Why are you doing this? Is it money? I can give you money.'

Right now she would happily pay a million euros for a hot shower.

'All in good time. You have twenty minutes.'

Megan stepped into the bathroom. The door locked behind her. The blindfold was easy to remove. She looked around the small bathroom. There were no clues suggesting its location. The room could be anywhere. There was a sink, a toilet and – yes! – a shower. On a stool she found knickers, a vest and a kind of kimono, all of them white. Was the kimono some kind of clue? She took off her soiled clothes and put them into a plastic bag that seemed to have been left for the purpose. Then she had the best shower of her life.

THE BARBICAN, LONDON

The buzzer sounded.

'Are you expecting anyone?' Flick asked Luke.

'No. Maybe we should leave it.'

'But what if it's to do with Megan?'

Luke pressed the button that connected him to the building's front desk.

'Mr Kite?'

'Yes?'

'I have a Mr – how do you pronounce your name again, sir? – Trevelyan here to see you.'

A video monitor sprang into life and Luke saw the Special Branch man. He looked stern, unaware of the camera.

'Send him up, please.'

'What's this Ian like?' Flick asked.

'Apart from you and Megan, he's the only person in the UK that I really trust,' Luke told her.

'That's good,' Flick said, squeezing his hand. 'We all need people we can trust.'

Ian talked through the Burma situation with Luke.

'I'm seeing Stella Lock tomorrow morning. She should be able to tell me the full extent of KI's involvement in Burma. From what I can gather, we're talking about companies within companies, with employees working on a "need to know" basis.'

'I didn't think that was the way my dad did business.'

'Your father's been gone for several months. It may be

that things have moved on since then.'

'Talking of my father . . .' Luke told Ian about the latest phone calls from Celine Michel.

'I haven't had time to look into her,' Ian said. 'I don't want you going over to Nice. The timing of her calls is too much of a coincidence. And you're next in line to be kidnapped.'

'I know, but she says it's about my father.'

'I'll see what I can find out. But don't do anything yet.'

'Understood.'

'And, please, don't go anywhere near the media. The news blackout is a good thing. There are elections imminent in Burma. Publicity may be the main thing the kidnappers want. Involving the press will make rescuing Megan more difficult.'

'Agreed,' Luke said.

'Is there any chance that KI will just do what the kidnappers want?' Flick asked.

'No,' Ian said. 'Not a hope in hell.'

He left.

'What did Ian mean,' Flick asked, ' "you're next in line to be kidnapped"?'

Luke thought for a moment. He had to tell someone and he trusted Flick.

'Just before she was kidnapped, Megan signed half the company over to me.'

'So you're as rich as Megan?'

'In theory.'

'And there was me thinking I was getting on with the poor cousin who has nothing but good looks to offer.'

'I hope this doesn't stop you liking me,' Luke said.

Flick smiled. The English liked a little irony. Luke decided to take his chance. Flick was only two years older than him, he'd discovered. And she didn't seem to think that the age gap made any difference. So he kissed her. A short peck, but on the lips. She kissed him right back.

'I'm glad you didn't tell me you were rich before I started having feelings for you,' Flick said, when they broke apart.

She had a point. From now on, the size of his fortune would attract more girls than his looks or personality. Good thing he'd already met Flick.

Ten

'Once the door is closed, you can take off the blindfold,' the woman said. 'We've done a few things to make you more comfortable. There's food, and a blanket if you get cold.'

Megan could hear what sounded like the hum of an air conditioner in the distance. The air felt rancid, recycled.

'Where am I?' she asked.

'You'll find out in good time. We don't want to hurt you. When we explain why we're doing this I hope you'll understand. Are you well? Do you need any medication for anything?'

'Not at the moment,' Megan said.

The woman left. Megan took off the blindfold. While she was washing, Megan's cell had been cleaned. It smelled of disinfectant. The space was maybe three metres square. There was a chair, a table, three copies of *Hello* and a Gideon Bible. The narrow, metal bed had fresh sheets.

It wasn't a room, as such. More like a container, with metal walls, like you got on the back of lorries. Megan sat down and picked up a magazine. She'd have swapped all three *Hello*s for a copy of *Private Eye*, but anything was better than nothing. Megan read about the wedding of a minor celebrity and the divorce of a distant royal. The door opened.

This kidnapper didn't wear a mask. He was good-looking. Mixed race. Dark, curly hair. Deep voice. He might be the guy in the messenger outfit who kidnapped her. She couldn't be sure.

'I'm Henry,' he said. 'I want to tell you why you're here.'

He talked about Burma for several minutes. The way he explained the BMFF's motivation made sense. At least it did if you thought that kidnapping ever made sense. Megan hid her anger. She acted weak, indecisive.

'What do you want me to do?' she asked.

'Tell KI to withdraw from Burma.'

'And then you'll let me go?'

'We'll let you go as soon as KI do what we ask.'

'But what if they don't?'

'They'll have to. You're in charge.'

'I don't know how much power I really have. I just turned eighteen. I haven't had my first meeting with the chief executive yet.'

'Listen.' Henry crouched next to her, gave a warm reassuring smile and patted her knee. Then he took her hand and squeezed it. 'Nobody's going to hurt you. We're all on the same side here. Can't we be friends and work this out together?'

'Sure,' Megan said, keeping her voice calm. 'Why not?'

LONDON

Flick rang Luke at eleven in the morning and asked if he'd made his mind up about going to Nice.

'I'll come with you if you want,' she said.

Of course he wanted. He was anxious to meet Celine Michel, and to spend more time with Flick.

The conversation with Ian Trevelyan was brief.

'KI have given us a vast amount of information on their operations in Burma,' he told Luke. 'I'm sifting through it now.'

'Did you find out anything about Celine Michel?'

'Nothing damaging. You say she won't come to the UK?'

'She can't travel, for some reason.'

'That's the suspicious thing.'

'I want to go and see her,' Luke said. 'What she has to tell me might be linked in to what's happening to Megan.'

'I doubt that.'

'You're sure that Megan's safe?'

'Members of this group have only ever used non-violent action. They're very unlikely to hurt her.'

'If we're talking days rather than hours, I think I should go to Nice, see Celine Michel. Find out what she has to say.'

'We've nothing on her but I still advise against it, Luke. If you do decide to go, please keep me in the loop. I can put Interpol on alert, in case you run into any trouble.'

Luke made the decision. He had to step up and take charge of the situation. No one else could. He rang Celine to tell her that he was on his way. Then he phoned Flick back. She was online and used her KI credit card to buy plane tickets.

'I booked us hotel rooms too,' she explained in the check-in queue at Heathrow. "Our rooms aren't extravagant, but they should be nice. Megan uses the chain a lot,' she added. 'I've booked two stays with them later in the year.' Flick grimaced.

Tentatively, Luke put his arm around her.

They were both thinking about whether Megan would get a chance to use those reservations.

Luke gave Flick the lightest of kisses. She pulled away. Luke couldn't help but ask a question.

'Does it bother you that I'm two years younger than you?'

Flick gave him one of her gentle smiles. 'I've never been out with anyone younger than me before. I guess I'll have to order the drinks, do the driving, pay for stuff. It sounds kind of cool. How do you feel about having an older girlfriend?'

'It feels kind of cool, too,' Luke admitted. 'But I wish we'd met in different circumstances.'

'If the circumstances were different, we wouldn't have been thrown together like this,' Flick pointed out. 'There's no need to feel guilty, but let's take it slow. OK?'

'OK,' Luke said. He'd not had a proper girlfriend before. He found it hard to trust women. He had a hard time trusting anybody, except for Andy, his closest friend, who he sometimes stayed with in Brooklyn. Yes, he had feelings for Flick. But he found it hard to trust his feelings, too.

ISLINGTON, LONDON

Ethan strode into Grace's room without knocking. He looked angry.

'Luke's left the country,' he told Grace.

'What's the surprise? He lives in Brooklyn, not here. So he's gone home.'

'He's not gone home. He's gone to France, with Flick.'

Grace rolled her eyes. 'Flick wouldn't go for Luke.'

'Exactly. When did you hear of an eighteen-year-old girl falling for a sixteen-year-old boy?'

'I expect they're just friends,' Grace said. It wasn't a good idea to mention to Ethan that she found Luke rather attractive, in a sullen, intense, he-doesn't-know-what-he's-got-but-one-day-he-will way. 'Why do you think they've gone to Paris? To shop?'

'According to Trevelyan, they've gone to Nice, not Paris. He'll be heading for Cannes, the Riviera.'

Grace shrugged. 'Why are you getting so het up about it?'

'Because Luke ought to be leading the search for Megan, not romancing the staff.'

'Instead of complaining about Luke, we should be trying to help,' Grace suggested. 'Do we know anyone who belongs to a group that campaigns about Burma?'

Ethan sat on the edge of his sister's bed. 'Panya might,' he said, sheepishly.

Panya was a tall, beautiful girl with an Asian mother and English father. Ethan had dated her before he went to Africa for his gap year. Grace used to like her. So did Ethan, a lot.

'Have you stayed in touch with her?'

'We met for a drink a couple of months ago, when I got back to the UK. I think she was a bit cut up that I'd been back five minutes and was already seeing Megan.'

'Do you think she'll help?'

'There's only one way of finding out.'

Eleven

Today, if Megan had kept track of the days accurately, was the third anniversary of her mum's death. Megan had been away at school when it happened. She'd wanted to stay home but she was in her GCSE year and the cancer was progressing slowly. Then Mum deteriorated very suddenly. Mrs Duncan came to see Megan in her dorm early one morning. That dreadful, light knock on the door. When she saw the Head standing there, Megan knew at once what had happened.

You can't prepare for death. Megan was shattered. Dad was inconsolable, his grief made worse by guilt. He hadn't always been a great husband. Even during Mum's illness, he worked away a lot. Early in their marriage, when Megan was a baby and Dad was away in the US all the time, building up the business, he had the brief affair that led to Luke's birth. Somehow he and Mum managed to get over that. According to Dad, their marriage became stronger as a result. In the months after Mum's death, Megan had to stay strong for him.

Megan tried to keep her grief under control. Only Grace saw how badly she took the loss. Megan was starting to get over the worst, or at least come to terms with it, to remember the good times. Then Dad died.

And now this.

'Are you all right, Megan?' Henry asked when he visited at some indeterminate time. 'You seem a bit down.'

'I'm OK.' Hang tough, Megan told herself. These guys are deluded do-gooders. They're not going to hurt you.

'What's on your mind?'

'I'm going stir crazy,' she said. 'It's been – what? – three days. Could I have a TV, or a newspaper at least?'

'There's nothing about you in the media, I'm afraid. KI have secured a news blackout. After your uncle's actions earlier in the year, I expect they'll do anything to avoid bad publicity.'

'I don't want to read about myself, I want to know what's going on in the world.'

'I'll see what I can do.' Henry began a lecture on Burma, and all the injustices that take place there. Megan half listened. She nodded in the right places. She accepted the argument. Clearly, companies like hers shouldn't be helping out a corrupt, dictatorial regime. That didn't mean Megan could stop it happening, especially not from here. How would Stella Lock respond to the BMFF's threats? Not too well, Megan suspected.

'Would you like some gum?' Henry proffered a packet.

'Thanks a lot,' Megan said, unwrapping a stick. She hated gum.

When he was getting up to go, Henry squeezed her arm in an affectionate way.

'We really want you with us,' he said. 'It would mean a lot if you were fully on board.'

Megan gave him a weak smile. Was he coming on to her?

Did he really think that this was the way to seduce someone, personally or politically? She already had a boyfriend. What would Ethan make of the way this group was behaving?

Henry grinned. 'Everything's going to be all right,' he said, like a parent talking to a sick child.

When he'd left, Megan spat out her gum. She didn't trust Henry at all. But she hoped he was starting to trust her.

ISLINGTON, LONDON

Ethan messaged his ex, Panya: NEED SOME HELP. CAN WE MEET AT MINE? He felt awkward about seeing Panya, but had no choice. She was his only way in to the Burma activists. Would she talk to him? Ethan and Panya had met only once since he came back from Africa, early. She'd played it cool but it was obvious she still had feelings for him. As he did, for her.

Panya always knew he was going to Africa and didn't do long-distance relationships. Even so, she'd let him know that she hadn't seen anyone while he was away. She'd been hoping they'd start up again. But for Megan, they might have done. So this was bound to be awkward.

Panya replied within the hour. CAN COME TOMORROW.

Ethan confirmed the meeting. A few minutes later, Mum got in from work. The House of Commons was still in recess so she had time on her hands.

'What news?' he asked.

'About Megan?' I'm not directly connected, Ethan. There's no reason for Special Branch to keep me in the loop.'

'Mum, she's my girlfriend. She's Grace's best friend. She's an orphan and she's been living here for months. If we don't have a right to ask, who does? Luke? He's too busy romancing Flick in France. It's driving me bonkers. Thanks to the news blackout, it's like Megan doesn't exist!'

Mum apologized. 'You're right. I'll call Ian now.'

'Put it on speaker, please.'

Mum got through to the Special Branch officer straight away. 'This is Florence Thompson. My son Ethan is also on the line. Can you give us the latest on Megan's kidnap, Ian?'

'It's not good, Mrs Thompson. KI have given me plenty of information about their dealings in Burma, but they've redacted key information ·because they've signed confidentiality agreements with the Burmese government.'

'That's preposterous!'

'It gets worse. According to Stella Lock, the acting CEO, not only is some of the information about KI's activity redacted, but there are other parts of it that even she can't access. The subcontractors doing the work aren't KI employees. They're employed directly by the Burmese government. It's the kind of system multinationals use when they want to make money in countries that have sanctions against them.'

'Then who knows what KI are really doing in Burma?'

'Only one person, and he isn't talking. Mike Kite.'

Twelve

Exercise. Megan didn't know when she'd be allowed her next shower but, never mind, she worked up a sweat. Press-ups. Stretches. Squats to strengthen her legs. When the time came, she needed to be strong.

'Are there many of you in the BMFF?' Megan asked Henry when he brought her supper: a sandwich, a fresh bottle of water, and some reading matter. 'Here, I mean.'

'We're a tight unit.'

'You're not going to tell me where we are, or how many of you there are, are you?' she teased.

He smiled and shook his head. 'Read the article in *Time*. It shows how the generals are in bed with the drug traffickers.'

Henry left. Megan listened carefully. Didn't sound like there was anybody outside. Henry couldn't be alone in this building, wherever it was, but, if she found a way to get out of her cell, she might have a chance of running for it. Any chance was better than none.

Ignoring the sandwich, she resumed her exercises.

NICE, FRANCE

The city spread out ahead of them. Luke leaned over Flick, in the window seat, to get a good look. The plane flew in low, tracking alongside the seafront. Above them was a deep blue sky. Below, on the beach, Luke could make out several topless sunbathers. You didn't get those on Coney Island.

This was an expensive town. The short taxi-ride to the hotel cost nearly as much as the forty-five-minute run from Manhattan to JFK airport. Luckily, Flick had enough euros left from her last trip abroad with Megan.

Once they were settled into their adjoining rooms, Luke rang Celine. He let the phone ring and ring, but there was no reply. He looked at a map the hotel had provided. Luke expected Celine to live in one of the seafront tower blocks that dominated the city skyline. From the map, however, it looked like she lived at the back of the city's old quarter. He suggested to Flick that they get a taxi there.

'We'll need to get some euros first. That taxi used up all of my notes. It's probably quicker by bus or tram anyway. Why don't we explore a little first?'

'I dunno,' Luke said. He was here on a mission.

Flick bounced on the bed. 'C'mere!' she said. They embraced. 'Listen, there's nothing you can do about Megan tonight. Celine isn't in. You'd be far better off seeing her in the morning when you've had a proper time to relax. Trust me.'

Luke trusted her. She massaged his back and one thing led to another. Luke couldn't believe his luck. For a while, he

63

was able to forget about what was happening to his sister.

By the time they got out on to the seafront, it was eight. The sunbathers and swimmers were all gone. They joined the parade of locals and tourists promenading along the wide footpath. Sections of the stony beach appeared to belong to hotels, while others were taken up by restaurants. There was a little breeze. A man managed to cross all six lanes of highway on roller skates without stopping once. Flick consulted the fold-up map the hotel had given them.

'We're just along the coast from Cannes. Can we go?'

'Not this time,' Luke said. He turned over the sheet to look at the detailed street map. They located where they were.

'The old town starts over there. Let's go and take a look.'

The couple crossed the road, went under some archways and found themselves in a thriving restaurant area. They weren't hungry yet, so walked up cobbled streets to a pretty square in front of a closed cathedral. The streets were narrow but not claustrophobic. The place had character. Luke imagined his father would have liked it here.

Now he had his bearings, Luke looked at the map again. The area where Celine lived was a long walk. Too late to call. Or was it? Nearly nine in the evening. The restaurants were starting to get busy. Most people were eating on tables outside.

'Suddenly I'm starving,' Flick said. 'It's the sight of all this good food.'

They found a busy alleyway full of restaurants and chose one that had lots of seafood. Flick chattered away throughout the meal, keeping Luke distracted from Megan's situation, from Burma, from whatever it was that Celine had to tell him.

Flick wasn't shallow, but she stopped him from getting too deep. She had the ability to take life as it came, to live in the moment. What was she doing with Luke? The money? So far, she had paid for everything. Or, at least, the company had. Before leaving London, Luke had phoned Stella Lock, who was too busy to meet him but had spoken to him briefly on the phone. He'd requested his own company credit card and been promised one within twenty-four hours. It would be messengered to the hotel as quickly as possible, Stella assured him.

It seemed that Flick simply liked him for who he was. Girls had come on to Luke before, and he'd messed around with them a little. But they'd been younger girls, slightly silly girls. Flick might be light-hearted, but she wasn't silly. Why wouldn't he let himself believe his luck?

'That was delicious,' Flick said. She refused dessert and requested the bill in French, which impressed Luke. 'Where shall we go now?'

Luke looked at his watch. 'Wherever you want,' he said.

They walked back from the old town into the new, through a massive square with a huge fountain and endless figures on high plinths. The statues resembled plastic versions of Rodin's 'The Thinker', only lit up like multicoloured jelly babies. Luke and Flick ended up in a fancy bar on the front, playing pinball. Flick might have good French, but Luke could trounce her at pinball. He won every game. They walked back along the front to the hotel a little after midnight, holding hands all the way.

'Monsieur Kite?' said the concierge.

'That's me.'

'A message for you.'

Luke took the folded piece of paper. It contained an address he already knew and a message. *Mme Michel asks you her meet at 10.30 a.m. tomorrow. Come alone.*

'*Come alone*,' Flick repeated. 'Isn't that a little bit creepy?'

'She's obviously paranoid about something,' Luke said.

'Whatever. But you take care. I suppose it gives me the chance to go shopping.'

Luke smiled indulgently. His life had been so heavy for so long. Megan's kidnapping had made things even heavier. Right now, Flick was just what he needed.

Thirteen

This evening, Henry looked tired. He let his film clips do the talking: several news reports, and a documentary about the treatment of the Kachin people in northern Burma. He picked up his laptop, which he'd been using to show the video footage.

'I'd better let you get some sleep.'

'Thanks. Here, let me help you.' Having only one arm free, Henry was struggling with the heavy metal door. This was Megan's chance. The door was heavy and the door was open. She only had a moment to work out what to do. She tripped.

'Oh, sorry!' Megan said, falling into Henry, who let the laptop slip from his hands. Naturally, he jerked forward to try and catch it. Megan grabbed the key that was already in his hand, then kicked Henry from behind.

Henry rolled on to the floor, groaning. Megan darted outside the container, into a large, half-lit space. She pushed the door shut and thrust the bolt across.

The handle turned. A muffled voice said something that sounded like, 'Megan, don't be silly.'

It was too late to stop. She was committed. Megan slid the padlock into place and locked it. Then she looked around.

A large room, with what little light there was coming through a large, barred window.

She listened. Nobody was coming.

Henry began to bang on the door, so that would soon change. She needed to get out of here. Now.

Megan looked through the window. It was night. There were vast, unlit buildings opposite and beyond her. Warehouses, maybe, or old mills. An industrial area. She must be on the third or fourth floor. There had to be a way out.

She ran on to a landing. In the distance, footsteps. Loud conversation. Henry kept banging on the door. He made a serious amount of noise. Why hadn't she thought of doing that? Because they had told her that, whatever she did, nobody would hear her.

A staircase. Megan bounded down it, two steps at a time.

ISLINGTON, LONDON

'What happened to the front windows?' Panya asked, handing Ethan her soft, calfskin jacket. Since the kidnapping and the ransom demand, the windows had been replaced by shatterproof glass and their frames reinforced with iron bars. They looked very ugly.

'We're having increased security.'

Panya frowned. She had dark eyebrows and deep brown eyes. 'I heard your mum was promoted to the cabinet. Those police outside must be a pain, though.'

'They're not there all the time. Just this week.'

'Why? What happened?'

Panya probably hoped he'd invited her round as a prelude to their getting back together. And why wouldn't she think that? She was the best-looking girl he'd ever been with, no contest. And the cleverest.

Ethan explained the situation and watched her expression change. At first she was insulted. Then compassion kicked in.

'You poor thing! She was taken from your front door?'

'I feel so guilty,' Ethan admitted.

Panya hugged him.

'This isn't anything to do with *Free Burma Now!*,' she said. 'Sure, there are a few people who support bombing the military and government targets, but kidnapping? That's the sort of thing they do in Italy, or South America.'

'And now here. It's a small world. Megan's responsible for what's happening in Burma, so she gets taken in London.'

'What is it they say she's responsible for?' Panya asked.

Ethan swore her to secrecy about the whole deal, then went through what he had gathered so far.

'Our best guess is that KI has provided the Burmese military with the software and tech support to mount a massive surveillance operation on their entire society, or at least the part of it that has working telephones and computers.'

'And Megan Kite knew all about this?'

'No. She only inherited the company on her birthday, three days ago, the day she was kidnapped.'

'So what do you want from me?'

'Anything that will help.'

'I could ask around. What are the kidnappers' demands?'

'They want KI to withdraw from Burma completely and cancel all contracts.'

'Sounds like a good idea to me,' Panya said. 'Why not get KI to do what they ask? Then you'll get your girlfriend back.'

Fourteen

The warehouse was vast, its layout confusing. Megan got to the bottom of the stairwell but couldn't find a way out. She could barely see. Maybe she was in a basement and the exit was higher up.

At least she could no longer hear Henry, banging away three storeys above. Maybe that meant nobody else could.

She retraced her steps, then stopped. She heard a door open, saw a brief flash of light. A female voice.

'Hold on.' It was an educated voice. It could have belonged to someone she was at school with or one of Ethan's friends.

Megan pressed her body against the wall in case the speaker spotted her shadow. Then she listened carefully.

'That's better. Reception's OK out here. These old buildings are full of dead spots. Where did you say you are? Nice? What are you doing there?'

Pause for the answer, followed by a question.

'Phil's with her at the moment. He's got her twisted round his little finger. But that doesn't mean KI will play ball. And time's tight. Jim suggested we start cutting off body parts, send them to Stella Lock. I'm not sure if he was joking.'

Brief pause. Megan shuddered. She had learned that

Henry's real name was Phil and somebody called Jim was considering cutting off parts of her body if KI didn't cooperate.

'You're telling me that Luke is as important in KI as Megan is? That's worth knowing. It might change things.'

How did they find that out?

'What time? Yes, we have members over there. We should be able to organize something by tomorrow morning. Text me the address.'

The call ended. In the distance, the banging had started again. The woman remained in the stairwell. She yelled.

'Who's there?'

No reply. The woman went back into the room she'd come from. Before the heavy door closed on her, Megan heard her say: 'I think Phil might be in trouble.'

Megan daren't explore any further. She had to move fast. The best plan, she reckoned, was to hide on this floor until the other captors went up to investigate, then make a run for it.

But that would only work if she could find out where the exit was.

Megan tried a door to her left. Locked.

Above, the door opened again.

'He should be back by now.'

'He was going to show her some video clips.'

'That can't be him banging, can it?'

Megan tried another door. This one opened. She put a foot inside and it nearly went through the floor. The building was derelict. She prayed that her captors hadn't heard the crunch made by the wood splitting.

Footsteps sounded on the stairs. Megan waited for them to go into the room where Henry/Phil was locked up. Then she went back outside.

She shot down the stairs, on to what she hoped was the ground floor. The stairs were metal and she could hear her every step. Once, she missed her footing and nearly went flying, but she somehow managed to grab a side rail and right herself.

Where was the exit? Was this the basement again? Maybe she needed to go back up a floor.

She couldn't go back, because now there were more footsteps pounding the staircase above, coming quickly.

She needed to get out of the stairwell, fast.

She needed to find somewhere to hide.

NICE

Flick had gone to bed. They were in adjoining rooms. For a few minutes Luke had heard her talking to someone. Probably her parents. It was only ten, but she'd said she was tired. Luke was still wired. He thought about knocking on her door. But no, he mustn't push things too fast.

He wondered if there was any news about Megan. Who could he call? Luke remembered that he hadn't spoken to Ian Trevelyan. He'd promised to let the Special Branch man know if he went to Nice but had been worried he might try to stop him. Only fair to call him now.

Ian answered his mobile at once.

'Luke! I gather you're in Nice.'

'How do you know that?'

'We have our ways of keeping track of people. Anyway, thanks for calling. Have you met Celine yet?'

'No. Tomorrow morning.'

'I'll be interested to hear how that goes. There's no news on Megan, I'm afraid.'

'Aren't Kite Industries doing what the kidnappers ask?'

'Getting the information to complete a convincing withdrawal from Burma is proving difficult.'

'Are you sure they're not stonewalling you?'

'Some of the problem is to do with confidentiality agreements. Worse, much of the work was subcontracted to a company within the company, and they're effectively firewalled.'

'So how do we get hold of that information?'

'We've one chance. I've just obtained a visiting order to see Mike Kite in prison in upstate New York.'

'Mike won't talk to you.'

'It's our only chance of getting the full story,' Ian said. 'I have to take it.'

'No,' Luke told him. 'I've got a better idea. Mike still thinks I'm his son. Let me go see him. If I ask the right way, I think I can get him to give me the information we need.'

'You're willing to fly to the US tomorrow?'

'After I've seen Celine, yes.'

'That's very brave of you. I'll get a flight booked and prepare you a briefing paper. Sure you can handle this?'

'There's only one way to find out.'

Fifteen

Megan had no idea what time of day it was. Morning. Afternoon. It could still be night for all she knew. The day they took her, she wasn't wearing a watch and, when she came to, they had taken her mobile. Last night, she had scurried into this dark, vast space, which was a nightmare to get around. There were wires everywhere, holes in the floor and several raised platforms where, at some point, industrial machinery stood. She had bruised her knees and fallen several times before finding her hiding place, a chest. It was dusty but empty. The chest was half hidden by some oily tarpaulin. She'd scrambled into it shortly before a search party went through the room. That was hours ago. The air in the chest was getting congested. She had slept a little but was very uncomfortable and badly needed a pee. It must be light by now. In daylight, surely she could find a way out.

Cautiously, Megan pushed up the chest's tin lid, letting in musty, oily air. She grabbed at the tarpaulin and pulled back enough of it to see daylight. Then she raised herself up using the side of the chest. Dust filled the air, and she tried not to sneeze. Her body was stiff and aching so it took her what felt like an age to pull herself out of the metal chest. She lifted her legs over the sharp rim, then stood on the greasy floor and looked out of the huge, iron-barred windows opposite. She saw that she was on the ground floor. Freedom was only a few metres away. All she had to do was find something heavy to smash through the windows. She could make a clean getaway. Or perhaps there was an easier exit. Megan looked behind her.

'Ah, there you are,' Henry said. 'I thought you must be hiding in here somewhere, but I didn't want to disturb your beauty sleep.'

NICE, FRANCE

Flick accompanied Luke through the old town, where stores were starting to open. They passed one that sold nothing but umbrellas. Another, four times the size, was devoted to men's hats. Flick wanted him to try on a Panama hat but Luke didn't have time. He kissed his girlfriend goodbye.

'I'll call you when I'm through with Celine,' he said, and headed uphill.

The roads grew a little wider, the buildings a little newer, each one painted a different pastel shade. He overshot the road where Celine lived, but found it in the end, near a wide, winding boulevard with signs for the Matisse museum. It was a pedestrian-only street, with concrete bollards on one side and, on the other, remote-controlled metal poles that went down when residents needed to park their cars.

The apartment itself was above a narrow archway. The first floor, where Celine lived, had a terrace with potted plants and black iron railings. One of the windows, unusually, had white net curtains for privacy. The nets were on the outside, between the window and the shutters. They were partially pushed out, presumably by an open window.

The buzzer read *Michel*. Luke pressed it.

'*Oui?*'

'*Je suis* Luke Kite,' he said, using approximately ten percent of his total French vocabulary. She buzzed him in.

At the top of a narrow stairway, Celine opened the door. The sunlight from behind her was so bright that he was momentarily dazzled. He shook her pale, cool hand.

'Hello, Luke,' Celine said, and began to cry.

'Are you OK? Is something wrong?'

'No, no. It's only, you look so like your father. Forgive me.'

She took a linen handkerchief from a skirt pocket and wiped her eyes. Celine was his mom's height, on the small side. She reminded Luke of his mom before she had all the plastic surgery. Pretty, with a petite figure. Or what would have been a petite figure, were she not several months pregnant.

'The baby,' Luke blurted out. 'Is it . . . ?'

'Your father's. You're going to have a little brother.'

This was why she wanted him over here, to see for himself. If Luke and Megan had received the news in London, the situation would have been abstract, another complication to add to the Kite Inheritance. But here, with Celine in front of him, he felt overwhelmed. He was no longer his father's youngest child.

'Can I . . . can I touch?'

'Of course.'

He felt Celine's warm tummy.

'Now I know why you didn't want to travel.'

'There is more,' Celine said. 'But first, let me get you something to drink.'

They had iced tea; one of Dad's favourite drinks, she said. She was probably right, but Luke said nothing. He didn't want Celine to find out how little he knew his father.

'Did Dad know that you were pregnant?' he asked.

Celine shook her head. 'He was supposed to be coming to see me the day after the crash. I meant to tell him then. I had only just worked out that I was a few weeks gone.'

'Did Dad want more children?' Luke asked. It wasn't a subtle question, but he needed to know.

'We hadn't discussed that,' Celine said. 'He knew that I wanted children. He said how much pleasure you and Megan had given him over the years, how much satisfaction.'

That didn't sound like Jack Kite, but Luke let it pass. If you'd lost the father of your unborn child in a helicopter crash, you were bound to idealize him. The dead didn't let you down by forgetting birthdays, or not calling from one month to the next.

'I thought,' Celine went on, 'that is, I hoped, that we'd marry, do all those happy family things. Maybe we still will.'

'What?' What was she on? Pregnancy did strange things to people, Luke knew. Hormones messed around with the mind.

'Don't look at me that way,' Celine told him. 'I'm not crazy. I want to play you your father's last message to me.'

Sixteen

Luke was shaken by hearing his father's voice on the answering machine. The message left him convinced of two things. His father had been fond of Celine, there was no question of that. And Jack Kite knew he was in danger from within his own family. The message didn't convince Luke that Dad was still alive. He tried to explain this to Celine. It was hard to do tactfully. Luke had only met her a few minutes ago. He felt shy in her presence.

'When my sister was in Tokyo somebody convinced her that Dad was still alive. But that was just a way to get to her. She was nearly killed.'

'Where is Megan? I thought she might come with you.'

'No.' Luke explained the situation.

'This must connect to what happened to Jack!' she insisted.

'I don't think so. I don't want to sound cruel but . . . you haven't heard from Dad since the helicopter crash, have you?'

'No,' Celine admitted.

'We know who shot the helicopter down. A man called Graham Palmer. He was working for Dad's brother, Mike. Wreckage was found in the ocean. Dad couldn't have survived. It's sad, but it makes sense. Dad being alive and not contacting you, or me, or Megan – that doesn't make sense.'

Celine stared at him. Luke saw a sharpness in her sad eyes. The superficial resemblance to his mother had led Luke to think of Celine as another dumb blonde, but she was much more.

'Listen to the message again,' she said, and pressed *play*.

'*Darling, I'm taking my daughter out to dinner tonight as an end-of-exams treat. Then I'll fly to you in the morning. I wish you were here. There's something I need to warn you about. It may come to nothing but there are people who want me out of the way. I don't want you involved in any of this. If the situation gets bad, I may have to disappear for a while. Should that happen, don't lose faith in me, and whatever people say happened to me, don't believe it. I have a lot of enemies, some of them very close to home. Remember, everybody lies. Even family. Until tomorrow, chérie. I'll call when I'm on my way.*'

'It proves nothing,' Luke said, hesitantly. 'I wish it were otherwise, but . . .'

'And what about this?' Celine said, handing him a postcard. The writing looked like Dad's. There was only one word in the space for the message: *Come!*

'You think this is from my dad?'

'What else can I think?'

Luke turned the card over. The card showed the Byron Hotel in Athens, Greece. It was the sort of card that hotels gave away, rather than one you bought. He examined the postmark. The card was sent only a week ago.

'This is a place where we stayed once,' Celine said. 'A

small hotel by the Parthenon. I want you to go there. Find Jack. Explain why I can't travel. Ask him to get in touch with me.'

'It's a wild goose chase,' Luke said.

'What does that mean, *wild goose chase*?' Celine's English was so good that he'd assumed she understood idioms too.

'You're trying to catch something that's impossible to catch because it doesn't exist. This writing could be anyone's.'

'It looks like your father's.'

'It looks a bit like his writing on birthday cards, but it can't be. Could it be an old boyfriend of yours? Or a relative? Someone you've forgotten about.'

'Please!' Celine begged. 'Take the card. Have the handwriting analyzed. If it is your father's writing, go to Greece for me. Look for him. Will you promise to do that?'

Luke couldn't see a way out of this. 'If experts say that the writing's my dad's, then, of course—'

His phone rang. He was relieved to be interrupted. The display read *Ian*.

'Excuse me,' Luke said and took the call.

'Luke? Have you seen Celine yet?'

'I'm with her now. She's convinced . . .'

He quickly told Ian what Celine had told him.

'We can discuss that when you're back in London. Are you still willing to fly to the US to see your uncle?'

'Yes, of course.'

'There's a ticket waiting for you at Nice airport. If you can get there within the hour, there's a connecting flight to Charles De Gaulle. You'll be just in time for a flight to JFK. I have a man from Interpol on hand to collect you at Celine's.'

'I'll need to go back to the hotel first, get my stuff, see Flick. Can she come with me?'

'Not a good idea,' Ian said. 'Too many security issues.'

Luke didn't want to explore that now. He doubted, anyway, that Flick would want to go to New York to visit his jailbird uncle.

'The car will be with you in a few minutes,' Ian said. 'I'll prepare an electronic briefing pack for you to read on the plane.'

Luke told Celine why he had to go. 'I'll be in contact as soon as I get back to London. But you must understand that I need to discuss this with Megan before I can work out what to do about . . .' he waved his arm a little to signify his missing father, the bump in Celine's belly '. . . all this. OK?'

They hugged awkwardly.

'Take good care of yourself,' he said, then left to wait for his car. The street was quiet. He got out his phone to call Flick. She wouldn't be happy that he was leaving without her. He'd have to sweet-talk her. He wasn't sure he knew how to.

No need. The call went straight to answering service. She was probably trying on clothes. He left a message explaining the situation.

'I'll see you back in London,' he finished. 'Please wait for me at the Barbican flat. I'll only be a couple of days.'

'Monsieur Kite?'

That was quick. Luke slid the phone into his pocket and turned around. He thought it would be his driver, who didn't have enough space to get the car into the narrow street. But it wasn't. He turned to face a tall man in aviator sunglasses and a baseball cap.

'Yes?'

The man punched Luke hard in the stomach.

Luke fell to the ground, winded, in agonizing pain.

ISLINGTON, LONDON

Panya invited herself round, saying she had something to tell Ethan.

'How serious are you and Megan?' she asked him.

Best to underplay his feelings.

'We've only been seeing each other for a few weeks,' he replied. 'She's been through a lot – her dad dying, people trying to kill her. We've become close but it's too early to say how serious we are about each other.'

'It's kind of ironic, isn't it? They've kidnapped the richest teenage girl in the world, only they don't want money.'

'I'm not with Megan because of her money,' Ethan pointed out. 'She's my sister's best friend. There was always something inevitable about our getting together one day.'

'Inevitable?' He wished he hadn't said that. He wasn't even sure if it was true.

'Actually, I didn't really notice her as a girl until she changed her hair colour. Does that make me shallow?'

'Not really. Just male.'

'The thing is, I can't hang around waiting for KI to see if they can find a way to meet the BMFF's demands. I have to do something.'

'That's why I came round. There's a meeting tomorrow, in Notting Hill. There might be some people there who know something. I'll make a couple of calls.'

'Can I go with you?'

'Of course.' She gave him a look that mixed pity with affection.

'Are you seeing anyone?' he asked and he detected a flicker of satisfaction. She was glad he wanted to know.

'Nothing serious,' she said. 'I know you had good reasons for calling it a day, but you were my first, and I took it hard. I kept thinking that when you came back, we'd start over. Only . . .'

Only he had flown halfway round the world to rescue a friend of his sister's and fallen for her instead.

'I'd better go,' she said. 'I'll find out about this meeting, phone you soon.'

'Thanks.' He kissed her on the cheek and she pressed her body firmly against his in a half-hug. Then she was gone. Ethan phoned Ian Trevelyan.

'I got through to Luke,' Ian told him. 'He's flying to New York to see his uncle. He's our best hope now.'

Seventeen

'Aren't you going to give me my daily lecture?' Megan asked, when Henry returned to her cell. He had no laptop with him this time, and kept his distance from her.

'What would be the point? You've heard all of our arguments and still tried to escape.'

'You'd respect me less if I didn't try to escape.'

'What you did could have consequences for other people.'

'How do you mean?'

Henry didn't reply. Megan had been mulling over the phone conversation she'd heard while free, trying to interpret it. Who was on the other end of the phone? Who was in Nice? She had a terrible suspicion. Were the kidnappers planning to take Luke too? Her kidnapper stayed by the door.

'I told you there was no getting out of here. All you did was give everyone, including yourself, an uncomfortable night.'

'When am I going to be released?'

'Soon, I hope. But you'll have to help us.'

'What makes you think I'll do that?' Megan asked

Henry took a step forward and spoke in his soft, warm voice. 'I'm pretty sure that, deep down, you agree with us.

Obviously you won't agree with the way we brought you here. It's natural that you're upset about that. But you'll come round. We're good guys. We're right. One of these days, you'll see that.'

'Just because you're the good guys doesn't mean that you're right,' Megan said. 'Life's more complicated than that.'

NICE, FRANCE

Everything that happened happened very quickly. Another guy appeared. The two men grabbed Luke between them and frogmarched him under the arch beneath Celine's apartment. Ahead of them was a white van with its back doors open.

Luke was winded but managed to get his breath back enough to speak. 'Who are you?' he asked. 'The BMFF?'

They didn't reply. Had Celine set him up? The men had him gripped tightly by each shoulder. Luke had no chance of escape, unless he could summon help from a passer-by. But there were no pedestrians, no cars even.

Wait. There was a black saloon with shaded windows, coming down the road at speed.

The saloon turned suddenly, swivelling round to block the road between the men holding Luke and the white van they were dragging him to. Luke saw his chance.

'You'd better watch out!' he shouted. 'That's my bodyguard!'

One of the men hesitated, reaching into his pocket. For a

gun, probably. Had Luke just made things worse?

Luke kicked the other man in the ankle with the hard tip of his boot. He wrested himself away from the man pulling out the gun.

The saloon stopped. Its driver's side window wound down. Was this the guy Ian had sent to collect him?

Luke shouted a warning.

'They're armed!'

Then he ran.

One of the men pointed a long-barrelled revolver. Luke dropped to the ground. He ducked under the right side rear door of the white van. Then he rolled beneath the van. He was covered, but only for a few moments.

Luke got up and began to run. Glancing back, he couldn't see the person at the wheel of the saloon. But he could see the rifle that poked out of it, directed at his pursuers.

Luke stopped. The guy with the long-nosed revolver was about to point it at the saloon. He was too late. A bullet caught him in the arm.

He dropped the gun and swore, loudly, in English.

The rifle jerked upwards, pointing at each man in turn. The voice that spoke was English, but with a French accent.

'Stay where you are.'

The two men looked at each other. Luke looked at them. They were dressed identically, so much so that it would be impossible to tell them apart in an identity parade. The Frenchman shouted:

'Luke, get in the car now!'

Luke jumped into the back seat of the black saloon. As he got in, the driver got out.

'Stay there. You nearly got yourself killed just then!'

Luke watched while his saviour disarmed the two men then made them get into the back of the van, which he locked. He rejoined Luke in the saloon with the shaded windows.

'You're staying at the Mercure by the seafront, right?'

'Right.'

'Your plane leaves in just over half an hour. We'd better hurry.'

They set off, at speed. The man spoke into his radio in rapid French. Luke caught the word 'Interpol'. He seemed to be telling the police where to pick the kidnappers up.

'Did you find out who they were working for?' Luke asked.

'No. They would only have lied. Interpol will question them. I don't have time.'

'Who are you?'

'My name is Luc, same as yours. You must be a very important person, Luke Kite, for MI6 to send me to collect you. They did not say you were in such imminent danger, though.'

'I was visiting a woman who lived nearby. It's possible that she was the one who . . .'

Luke didn't finish the thought. He'd trusted Celine, told her about Megan. She even knew that he was co-owner of KI. Was she the one who had betrayed him to the kidnappers?

'We know who you were visiting,' Luc said. 'Leave it to us. You have an important job to do in New York.'

'I have to call my girlfriend,' Luke remembered.

If Flick was near the hotel, maybe they would have a chance to say goodbye.

The line was busy. They reached the hotel and Luc parked on the pedestrian zone outside. He escorted Luke up to his room.

Luke collected all of his stuff and scribbled Flick a note, explaining that he had to go.

Downstairs, at the desk, Luke left the note and explained that Flick would be leaving separately.

'OK. But wait. Monsieur Kite? You must sign for this.'

Luke was expecting a bill, but it was his KI credit card with a separate, sealed note giving him the PIN number and his credit limit, which had several noughts to it.

'Come on,' said the French agent. 'We have to get you to the airport.'

Luke kept an eye out for Flick all the way down the Boulevard des Anglais. But there was no sign of her.

Eighteen

'The generals slaughtered three thousand people in Rangoon in 1988,' Henry concluded. 'The West soon forgot about it. In 2001, terrorists blew up three thousand people in New York. In revenge, our country joined a war against a nation that wasn't even involved in the attack. Where's the fairness in that?'

'I feel ashamed that I didn't know about this,' Megan told Henry. 'Kite Industries shouldn't be in Burma. We have no right to help the generals. Let me out and I'll stop it, I promise.'

'How can we trust you?' Henry asked, his forlorn tone almost convincing. 'You tried to escape.'

'Why would I lie? I agree with you. I want to help. I understand why you kidnapped me. If I thought it was the only way to get through to KI, I might have done the same.'

'Good. Now we are getting somewhere.'

'So let me go!' Megan wanted to repeat, but she held her tongue. If and when they let her go, it would have to seem like their idea. She knew that much about psychology.

'What now?' she asked.

'While you're here, KI is under enormous pressure to withdraw from Burma. If that happens, the military junta will be greatly weakened. KI's withdrawal will effectively be a confession that allows us to expose the fraud the junta is perpetuating against the Burmese people. It will hasten the end of the regime. If the price to pay for such a result is your continued incarceration then I'm sorry, but so be it.'

'I understand,' Megan said. 'But what more do you want from me? I'm on your side.'

Henry nodded. 'If you swear, on your life, that you will not reveal who we are, then we *may* give you some more freedom. We don't ask that you join us, not yet, but to help us. Do you swear?'

'I swear,' Megan said, before she had time to think about what she was swearing to.

'Thanks,' Henry said. 'We're making progress. Come with me. There's something we want you to do.'

BROOKLYN, NEW YORK

Andy greeted Luke at the door of his brownstone home.

'Dude! It's been a while.'

'I know. Some things caught up with me in London.'

'Are you here to stay? Or are you going to use the apartment in the Village?'

Crystal, Luke's mom, had a flashy apartment in the Village. Mike Kite had paid a year's rent in advance. Luke could use the apartment when he wanted, but had been staying with Andy's family since he returned to the States. He still had a few friends around Brooklyn, but none in Greenwich Village.

'I don't know what I'm doing, Andy. Except that I'm here to see Mike.'

'Isn't he in a supermax upstate somewhere?'

'Yep.' His uncle was judged a danger of flight or escape and had been incarcerated awaiting trial in Clinton, one of New York's super maximum security prisons. Luke had a pass to visit him tomorrow. Then he would return to London.

After bringing Andy up to speed, Luke called the KI office in Manhattan.

'Luke Kite here. I think the security division are expecting me to call.'

'Of course, sir. Please hold the line just a moment.'

For the next few minutes, Luke was treated like royalty. Was it because he was an American that he was getting such different treatment? Or had news filtered through from London that, regardless of his paternity, Luke was an equal heir to the company? He was briefed about the next day's visit to Clinton, then put through to an old acquaintance.

'Is there anything else I can do for you, Mr Kite? asked Francis, who used to be his father's personal assistant. He now did the same job for Bethan Bracewell, who was in charge of the New York office. 'Shall I arrange for you to visit your mother? I can find out where she's being held.'

'I don't think so,' Luke replied. He hadn't seen Crystal since she lied to him about his paternity, just before Megan's 'funeral'. Mom had been complicit in all of Mike's crimes. Crystal wasn't clever enough to be part of them, but she knew the kind of stuff Mike got up to and she didn't mind. For all Luke knew, Mike's evil behaviour turned her on. The more Luke found out about his mother's secrets, the less he liked her.

Andy's mom returned from work while the two were playing video games. She gave her son's best friend a hug.

'But what are you doing here?' Jo Smith said. 'I thought you were staying in London for a week or two.'

'Things have changed.' Luke began to give her an edited version of events in London, but was interrupted by a phone call. Francis. A car would collect him tomorrow. Luke needed to phone Ian again, to go over the questions he had to ask.

When Luke got off the phone, both Andy and his mom looked serious. Something had been discussed while he was on the phone.

'What is it?'

'I'm sorry, Luke, but I don't think it's a good idea for you to stay here,' Jo Smith said.

'Why not?'

'Your cousin's been kidnapped. It's only a few weeks since Maria Delgado was killed by somebody working for your uncle.'

Maria had been mistaken for Megan, with tragic results.

'Andy tells me you're inheriting half the company. That makes you a target, Luke. A very big one. And a lot of people know you've been living here. That was OK while you were Luke Nobody, but now you need somewhere more secure. Don't think I'm being mean, but I have to look out for Andy and—'

'And yourself, of course,' Luke said. 'I wasn't thinking. I'll move into the Manhattan apartment tonight.'

'It can wait until tomorrow, dude,' Andy said. 'Nobody knows you're here yet.'

'I'm afraid they do,' Luke said.

He called Francis back, arranged for the car to pick him up in Greenwich Village the next day, adding, 'When I'm done out at Clinton, I may need to go straight back to the UK or – depending on where the conversation with Mike leads – I may hang around here a little longer. In which case I'll need some security at the apartment. I presume you heard what happened to my sister.'

'Yes, Mr Kite. Our full resources are at your disposal.'

'I'll be out of your hair soon,' he told Jo and Andy.

'You can always come and hang here,' Andy insisted.

'Thanks,' Luke said. He called for a cab. He wanted to call Flick, find out how she was, but that could wait until he got to the apartment. He and Andy made awkward conversation until the taxi arrived. Luke didn't tell him about Flick. Getting a girlfriend as a result of your sister being kidnapped didn't seem so cool somehow. Before driving off in the evening drizzle, Luke promised that, whatever happened, he would stay in touch with Andy.

'I'm sorry,' Mrs Smith said. 'You do understand, don't you?'

'Of course I do,' Luke said. 'I've got tons to thank you for. The last thing I want to do is put you in any kind of danger.'

'Be safe,' was the last thing she said to him.

He got into the cab, wishing he were Luke Nobody again.

Nineteen

GREENWICH VILLAGE, NEW YORK CITY

The apartment was on the second floor, what Brits called the first floor, which confused Luke sometimes. He had to remind himself that he was fifty percent a Brit. One day, he might feel as at home in parts of London as he did here. This rented apartment, five minutes' walk from Washington Square, hadn't been his for long. But it felt more like home than Dad's Barbican space did.

There was a light on in the living area, he noticed. Luke had set the timer himself, to deter prowlers. Good it was working. Easy to climb up the fire escape on the right, smash your way in if you were determined enough. Do that, though, and you'd set off the state-of-the-art security alarm.

When Luke opened the door, the alarm system didn't flash red at him. This situation was worryingly familiar. At the Barbican, when the alarm didn't sound, it was because Flick was in there, waiting for him. Megan had given her the code. But only two other people had the alarm code to this apartment, and both of them were in prison. Which meant . . .

Luke took in the polished wooden floor, the vast windows. He smelled coffee. Kidnappers and assassins didn't usually make coffee. The smell reminded him of the Brazilian Arabica blend that his mom always bought from a small store on Flatbush. He hadn't seen his mom since the funeral. She'd asked him to visit her in jail, but he'd felt betrayed. All those lies, all that greed. He'd thought he was better off without her. He still thought so. But here she was.

'Luke? Is that you, honey?'

Crystal appeared from the kitchenette. She held a ceramic mug with *World's Worst Drunk* in blurred letters on the side. Luke had given it to her last year as part of her thirty-fifth birthday present, an ironic joke which Crystal took in good humour, ignoring the mean side to Luke's intentions. For Crystal really liked a drink. Usually, though, she could hold her liquor.

'C'mere,' she said, putting down the mug. 'It's been months.' She covered his face with kisses. 'Let me look at you.'

While his mom was examining him, Luke got a good look at her. Crystal wore no make-up that he could discern. Her sweatshirt and jeans looked like prison issue. She had tiny, fresh lines around her eyes and, despite all the plastic surgery she'd had over the years, looked more like a real woman than the Barbie doll he had become used to.

'You've lost some of the fat in your face. You know, you're turning into a really handsome young man,' Crystal said.

Luke frowned. 'What are you doing here?' he asked. 'What on earth did you agree to do before they decided to let you out?'

'All in good time,' Crystal said. 'You've lost weight, too. Have you had dinner?'

'I've skipped a lot of meals recently,' Luke admitted.

'Then why don't we catch up while I make you some pancakes? You know how you love my pancakes.'

ISLINGTON, LONDON

Panya phoned Ethan.

'Has there been any word?'

'Nothing.' Ethan didn't tell Panya about Luke's New York trip. That stuff was classified.

'I've spoken to some people. It was tricky to explain, but I think they trusted me. I want you to join me at the *Free Burma* Now! public meeting in Notting Hill. There should be somebody there with BMFF connections. He's willing to talk to you.'

'Will you be there too?' he asked her.

'They want me there, yes, to vouch for you and guarantee that we weren't followed. But I think whoever it is will want to talk to you alone. This is serious, Ethan. I don't want to be arrested for being involved in kidnapping. I want to start university this month, not go to prison.'

'I appreciate the risk you've taken, Pan,' Ethan said. 'Did you find out anything else?'

'No. The whole thing's so tightly under wraps, the first few people I spoke to had no idea what I was on about. But they must have talked, because I got a phone call from someone I'd never met, then I was dragged to a secret meeting in a tower block in Camden. Man, that was scary.'

'I'm sorry. I really appreciate this – I do,' Ethan said.

'I hope she's worth it.'

GREENWICH VILLAGE, NEW YORK CITY

'Prison changed me,' Crystal told Luke, after they'd eaten. 'I used to feel hard done by. The women I met inside had so few choices, I felt like a spoiled brat.'

She paused, as though waiting for Luke to correct her.

'For the first time since you were born, I had no contact with Mike. He'd always been there, manipulating me, making promises, whispering poison, keeping me under his thumb.'

'How long were you and he . . .' Luke didn't want to discuss sex with his mother, but he needed to know when they stopped being lovers '. . . together?'

'Whenever he wanted us to be. Even if I was seeing someone else at the time. It never stopped, Luke. Your father has been the one constant in my life since you were born. But he was only using me. I see that now. To keep tabs on you. And, most of all, to get back at his brother.'

Luke bit his tongue. Seemed Crystal was convinced that Mike Kite, not Jack, was his father. Luke wanted to tell her the truth, but he had promised not to, and she had held out on him for long enough.

'Did you have any feelings for Jack Kite?' he asked.

'I adored Jack. But he was very married. He claimed that

he and his wife were having a trial separation at the time we had our fling. I don't know if that was true or not. Anyway, soon after we met, he introduced me to Mike. And anything Jack had, Mike had to have too.'

That was as much as Luke wanted to know. 'You still haven't explained why the authorities let you out,' he said.

'I didn't do anything wrong,' Crystal said. 'They tried to implicate me in the murder of that girl in Brooklyn, Maria Delgado, but I knew nothing about it until afterwards. I was at fault because I didn't go to the police when I began to understand what Mike had done. But after I agreed to testify against Mike, they dropped the charges.'

'You're going to be a witness against Mike? Don't you know how dangerous he is?'

'Not to me, he isn't. I'm the mother of his son.'

'Mom, Mike had his own brother killed!'

Crystal was unperturbed. 'I probably won't have to testify, the FBI said.'

'Why on earth not?'

'Because I can't tell the courts a thing that the FBI isn't able to prove a different way. What I have to do is figure out how to make a living, now I don't have money coming in from Mike or Jack. I want to support you through college.'

'Don't worry about that,' Luke said. She didn't know about his inheriting half of KI and he had no intention of telling her.

'I'll figure out a way. Mike paid for a two-year lease on this place. If the worse comes to the worst, I can sublet it and we can live somewhere cheaper.'

She thought he was going to live with her.

'How's Megan?' Crystal wanted to know. 'When I asked the FBI if you'd be home when I was released, they said you were in London for her eighteenth birthday.'

'She's fine,' Luke lied. 'It was a good party. But listen, I'm still on UK time, which means, according to my body clock, it's three in the morning. Can we talk more tomorrow?'

'Of course,' Crystal said. She hugged him. 'It's so good to be home, to see you again.'

Luke hugged her back. 'You're looking well, Mom.'

He went to bed but found it impossible to sleep. He'd blocked Crystal from his mind for so long. Now that she was back, it was impossible to keep hating her. She was his mom.

Tomorrow, he was to meet Mike, who he'd hoped never to see again. He had no idea whether Mike would tell him what he needed to know. Mike did nothing unless there was an advantage in it for him. Would he have any compassion for his kidnapped niece? Luke doubted it, given he'd tried to have her killed at least twice already.

Twenty

Megan's hair was brushed, but they had not allowed her any make-up. She was meant to look pale and a little scared. Not too scared. Those watching had to know that she agreed with what she was saying. She didn't have a gun to her head. She didn't want anyone to think she was suffering from Stockholm Syndrome, where kidnap victims began to sympathize with their captors and brainwashed themselves into joining their cause. Megan knew exactly what she was doing.

She looked into the camera.

'I have been taken because of Kite Industries' behaviour in Burma. The company I own is propping up one of the world's most abominable regimes, spying on its citizens and using new technology to limit their contact with the outside world, so that we can't see what terrible things are going on.

'I will only be freed if KI withdraws completely and unilaterally from Burma. It must also announce publicly that it will have no further contact with the country until there are democratic elections and the winners of these elections are allowed to govern.

'This is not a ransom demand. I know that the British government does not pay ransoms and I do not want KI to pay ransoms either. Paying kidnappers only encourages kidnappings. But my captors' cause is just. They have taken me because it is the only way to get the world's attention. So I ask that, after I am released, no attempt is made to track down my captors. In fact, as the owner of the majority of shares in KI, I order that no attempt is made to capture my kidnappers.'

She should have said 'co-owner' but Luke's involvement wasn't public knowledge. Or was it by now? Megan hesitated. The script had a paragraph left on it.

'One more thing . . .' she said.

CLINTON, NEW YORK STATE

The Clinton Correctional Facility dominated the upstate village of Dannemora, deep in the Adirondacks, a long drive from NYC. Luke had had time to memorize all of the questions Ian had given him. A cold wind whipped through the streets. The prison's long walls, sixty feet high, bordered the village's small business district. This was the biggest supermax in the whole state. And, Luke was willing to bet, the bleakest.

Luke got through security. The visiting area reminded him of the mess at his old school. Functional, boring, designed to depress. Mike was awaiting trial, not convicted, so Luke was allowed to meet him face to face, without direct supervision. Luke sat at a low table and waited for his uncle to be led in.

Mike had aged in the three months since his arrest. His

orange prison garb made his complexion look raw, mottled – or maybe that was the fluorescent lights overhead. There was more grey in his hair and he had bags beneath his eyes. The flesh beneath his chin had begun to loosen, which Luke had never noticed before. Mike was forty-three.

'Hello, son,' Mike held out his hand. Luke shook it.

'Good to see you, Mike.'

'How's your mom?'

Instant alarm. Did Mike know that Crystal was out?

'I haven't seen her.'

Mike seemed to accept this. 'I heard a joke the other day, made me think of Crystal. What accessories come with the new Divorced Barbie doll?'

This was one of the things that Mike and Luke had done since Luke was old enough to talk: simple knock-knock and question and answer jokes.

'I don't know, tell me.'

'All Ken's stuff.'

Luke laughed. The surface ice was broken.

'You must still hate me,' Mike said, changing the mood. 'What's so important that you came all the way to New York's Siberia in order to see me?'

'Megan's been kidnapped,' Luke said. 'By a group protesting about KI's involvement in Burma.'

'That's bad,' Mike said. He paused and allowed his face to form a token display of sympathy. 'I told Jack that working in Burma was a mistake. One that would come back to haunt us.'

'Burma was Jack's project, not yours?' That wasn't in the script. Luke's father was the good guy at KI. Everything

103

dodgy was down to Mike. The Burma operation had Mike written all over it. But Luke kept this thought to himself.

'Oh, I did most of the dirty work, as usual,' Mike said. 'What do the kidnappers want?'

'Complete withdrawal. Dismantling of the surveillance system that's about to become fully operational. No cooperation with the Burmese military whatsoever.'

'And what has KI's response been?'

'KI security's trying to track Megan down. The new CEO, Stella Lock, has made supportive noises, but says KI can't break contracts without incurring huge financial penalties.'

'That's bull. It's very hard for the Burmese government to impose penalties when they're the subject of so many sanctions. But if KI withdraw from Burma, other regimes in the area are much less likely to give us similar contracts in the future.'

'I don't care about that.'

'No, but Stella Lock will. If you want to get her on-side, your best bet is to argue that, should KI's involvement in Burma become common knowledge, the bad publicity could damage the corporation in all sorts of ways.'

'In that case, why get involved in the first place?'

'It's business. The profits are huge. So I set up a sham company to handle the most controversial stuff.'

'What's it called?'

'I don't recall. Why haven't I heard about this kidnap?'

'An injunction. There's been a total news blackout.'

'That's good. It means the kidnappers really do want to negotiate, they aren't just doing this to get on the news.'

'Megan's been gone for days now. I'm really worried.'

'Your cousin's a rich bitch, Luke. A little discomfort will do her good. That said, a little bird tells me that she cut you in to half the company. I can see why you'd be very grateful to her.'

'Who told you that?' Luke couldn't hide his surprise.

'I still have my sources, even here.'

They exchanged wary expressions. Mike had made it clear that he knew Luke was holding stuff back. He'd tried to get a rise out of him by criticizing Megan. How much did he know?

'What is it you want from me?' his uncle asked.

'I want information about KI in Burma. I need to know exactly what we're doing there. Then I'll tell Stella Lock that I'll go public unless she withdraws KI from all Burmese activities.'

'Stella's tough. She won't back down unless she has to. But sure, I'll tell you what you want.' He paused and looked Luke right in the eyes. 'Provided you promise to visit me again. It gets lonely up here. You're my only family.'

'I know,' Luke said. 'Of course, I'll visit.'

Mike hesitated. Then he spilled. 'OK. Here's the deal . . .'

Luke took notes. He was still taking notes when visiting time came to an end. Mike left him with a warning.

'You want Megan back safe and I hope you rescue her. But if she dies, and it's just you, there'll be a lot of people who want you out of the way. There's a long time before you get to your eighteenth birthday and have real power. Protect yourself.'

'I will.'

'Have you got a girlfriend?'

'Sorta. Her name's Flick. Blonde, very pretty.'

Was Flick really his girlfriend? Luke still felt like he had to impress Mike. Why? His uncle was a complete bastard.

'How old?'

'Eighteen.' Whatever Flick was to him, Luke missed her.

'When I was your age, I liked older women, too,' said Mike, his tone sleazy. 'I hope you're having a good time.'

They exchanged a handshake. Mike was led back out. Luke had conflicting feelings for his uncle. Hard to hate the only father figure who'd been around when he was young. Hard to reconcile the Mike he loved with the Mike who tried to have Megan killed. Who effectively murdered his own brother.

If Dad really was dead.

Whatever. Luke had come away with what he came for.

Twenty-One

'Did I do OK?' Megan asked Henry.

'You did more than OK. I hope that'll get you out of here.'

'How long have you been planning this?'

'Since word started to trickle through about what KI was up to in Burma.'

'I wish it had trickled through to me,' Megan said.

'At first we were going to kidnap your father,' Henry said.

Megan flinched but said nothing.

'Then we thought about taking you to put pressure on him instead. However, some of us weren't happy about the ethics of taking a schoolgirl. Then he died.'

'And I inherited the whole company.'

'And became responsible for everything KI does.'

'How can I be responsible when I was never told about it?'

'I don't have an answer for that. But it doesn't matter. You've taken responsibility now. You've stepped up.'

'And what's next?' Megan asked.

'After KI withdraws from Burma? We let you go, of course. But I hope that you'll join us,' Henry added. 'With you on our side, the BMFF would have every chance of meeting all its objectives much sooner than would otherwise be the case.'

'You want me to join you? To become a member of the BMFF?'

'It makes complete sense, doesn't it?'

'Yes,' Megan said, her will weakening. 'I suppose it does.'

NOTTING HILL, LONDON

Ethan hadn't been to the Portobello Road since he got back from Africa. There were bars and clubs he liked round here, some funky shops. But he had never been in this stuffy Salvation Army hall before. There were, at most, twenty people at the meeting. From what Mum told him, Special Branch had infiltrated this group, *Free Burma Now!*. Who was the mole? That bloke in the baggy sweater? The muscular skin with tats on his biceps? The big woman with tinted specs, showing more cleavage than was common in left-wing circles?

The real mole, of course, was Ethan himself. He didn't know what he was doing in this rundown hall, being introduced to pro-democracy activists. Panya didn't tell anyone his surname. They might make the connection with his parents.

Ethan didn't join in the discussion. Most of it was about fundraising activities. There was an upsetting report by the Karen Women's Organization detailing the ongoing rape, murder, torture and forced labour suffered by women living under the Burmese military regime in Karen State. Then, as light relief, there was a talk by a Canadian cartoonist. He had written and drawn a book about the time he'd spent living in Burma with his wife, who was working for a medical charity there. The talk was followed by questions.

'Could your book be sold in Burma?' somebody asked.

'No way. Censorship there is strict and I say a lot about the regime and how it operates.'

'Do you think the tourism embargo ought to be lifted?'

'No. Tourists say how welcoming the Burmese people are, how the people don't want the country to feel so isolated. But any growth in tourism helps the junta to pretend that things in Burma are normal. The junta's desperate for overseas aid, even more than for tourist dollars. And most aid goes straight into the dictators' pockets.

'The issues are complicated. Tourism brings some benefits to ordinary citizens. But there's something incredibly arrogant about Western tourists who think it's fine to visit a country even when they're asked not to by groups they claim to support. Unless the opposition position changes, I think that tourists who go to Burma share responsibility for the repression there.'

Panya poked Ethan in the side. 'Look!' she hissed. A handful of people were leaving early. 'Let's go.'

They followed the group at a distance, on to the street. The four men had left one by one but were getting into the same car, a four-door Ford Focus with a bad spray paint job.

'I was told to follow them,' Panya said.

'Do you know any of them?' Ethan asked.

'The tall one with the dreads is called Greg. He introduced himself to me once. I don't know any of the others.'

'Get his attention, please.'

Panya yelled Greg's name and hurried over to him. Ethan watched her speak rapidly, then point back to him. After a minute, she beckoned Ethan over.

'I explained about your girlfriend,' Panya said.

Greg gave Ethan a long, cool look.

'You go out with a rich chick who's been kidnapped?'

Ethan nodded.

'And why exactly do you think we can help?'

'I'm looking to make contact with a group called the BMFF. I don't want to make trouble for them. I just want to save Megan.'

'I see. Step back and wait a minute, will you?'

Ethan did as they asked. Greg had a confab with the driver and guys in the back. He summoned Ethan to rejoin them.

'Get in the back of the car,' he told Ethan.

'What about Panya?'

'There isn't room for her too.'

Ethan got in. The car began to move. The Asian guy squashed next to Ethan handed him a brown-paper bag.

'Put this over your head.'

'What? Why?'

'We can't have you seeing where we take you. Trust us or get out of the car.'

Ethan did what he was told.

GREENWICH VILLAGE, NEW YORK CITY

When he returned to the apartment, Luke started to write a long report for Ian. Crystal got back as he finished up. He decided to play it straight with his mom. He told her where he had been and why.

'I fly back to London later tonight.'

'Why do you have to go back to England?' Crystal asked.

'To be there for Megan.'

'You've done all you can by seeing Mike.'

'Give me a minute here, would you?'

Luke double-checked the information he had put into the email. Then he used an encryption programme. It was one of Jack Kite's but he had modified it slightly. Ian Trevelyan would be able to open the email with a code that Luke had given him, but nobody else would. And nobody would be able to read the email on this laptop either. He pressed *send*.

'Did Mike ask anything about me?' Crystal wanted to know.

'He thinks you're still in prison and I'm still having nothing to do with you,' he told her.

'He didn't talk about me at all?'

'No.'

'I really wish you'd stay.'

Luke hesitated. Crystal was his mother. He owed her something for bringing him up. She was about to testify against his uncle, which could create all sorts of danger. She didn't know that Luke was co-owner of KI, and he wasn't going to tell her. One day, he would be in a position to help her. Not yet.

'I have to go back to England. Hopefully not for long. I'll try to help you with the FBI. Do you have a lawyer?'

'Only a court-appointed one.'

'I'll see if there's any way I can get Megan to fund one through KI. But that'll only work if she's freed.'

'Thank you, honey.'

Now that Luke's return to the UK had an advantage in it for Crystal, she was happy to help him pack. She even drove him to JFK. Once she'd dropped him off, Luke rang Flick.

'I've missed you,' she said.

'I'll be back in a few hours. Wait for me at the Barbican?'

'I'm already here.'

They blew kisses to each other over the phone. Everything was going to be all right, Luke told himself. Things would work out for him and Megan. Maybe even for the people of Burma, too. Ian's briefing notes had made it clear that KI were helping one of the worst regimes in the world. Mike had confirmed that KI were helping the junta spy on their citizens. And, without being specific, he'd suggested that the company was about to do more to help the evil regime. Much more.

Twenty-Two

LONDON

The guy with the dreadlocks pushed Ethan into a dark space.

'Is this where you're holding Megan?'

'You have to wait,' the Dread said. 'Be patient.'

Ethan wasn't noted for his patience. He had to have everything straight away, as Megan often pointed out. He missed her badly. He'd do whatever it took to get her back safe and well. So he stood in the gloomy room, waiting. Where was he? At least he didn't have a bag over his head any more.

It might have been ten minutes before the Dread returned. It might have been half an hour. Ethan didn't wear a watch. He always used his mobile to check the time. They'd confiscated that. Probably gone through all his texts to check up on him. That was OK. There was nothing secret on there, nothing to contradict anything he'd told them in the car.

The door opened.

'Put this back on your head,' the Dread said.

Ethan put the bag back over his head, allowed himself to be frogmarched out of the building. He tried to count paces.

Ten . . . fifteen . . . he lost track after twenty. Then he heard another door open and close. The temperature became slightly warmer.

'I'm going to sit you down,' the Dread said. 'Relax.' It was like one of those trust exercises they do in Drama classes: allow yourself to fall back and believe that there will be a chair there.

There was.

A new voice spoke. Deep and warm.

'Can I trust you to keep that bag on your head or shall I have your hands tied behind your back?'

'You can trust me,' Ethan said.

'Tear the bag a little. Give him room to breathe.'

Somebody did as the new voice asked. That was better.

'Who are you?' Ethan asked.

'I am a liaison for the BMFF. That's all you need to know.'

'You're the people holding Megan?'

'Yes.'

'Is she nearby?'

'No. You are Ethan Thompson, son of a cabinet minister, former aid worker. I understand that you want to save your friend.'

'She's more than a friend.'

'Very well. But listen to this. Megan does not need saving. Am I right in saying that there are no plans to lift the news blackout imposed by the government?'

'Not as far as I know.'

'KI are scared of bad publicity because of their behaviour in Burma. Your girlfriend's company refuse to pull out because they would lose a lot of money. But they will be forced to. Your mother's government will tell them to. And so will Megan Kite. Soon, KI will have no choice but to do as we ask.'

'Megan's on your side?'

'Yes. She would have preferred not to have been held to ransom. But these are turbulent times. Personal freedom is a luxury that not even the rich can rely on.'

'What are you going to do with her?'

'As soon as KI can present us with proof that they have completely withdrawn from Burma, Megan will be freed.'

'And if they find it impossible to withdraw?'

'Then you will force us to take more severe measures.'

Ethan didn't like the sound of that. 'What do you want me to do?'

'Deliver this DVD to your mother and to Kite Industries.'

JFK AIRPORT, NEW YORK CITY

Luke's mobile rang twice while he was waiting to check in. Ian Trevelyan was in the UK, where it was the early hours of the morning.

'The information you sent was crucial. There are one or two things I want to go over with you . . .'

Luke answered the questions as best he could.

'That's incredibly helpful,' Ian said. 'There's one other thing that comes out of the police investigation into the kidnap and the kidnapper's note. It said *Megan was warned*?'

'I remember.'

'Did you notice any literature about Burma in the

Barbican or ever discuss anything like that with her?'

'No. Megan's not very political.'

'Some pro-democracy literature was found in the flat.'

'I didn't go through her stuff, so I don't know what to say.'

'OK, forget it for now. Have a good flight. We'll talk again tomorrow. Again, thanks for doing this, Luke. I know it must have been very awkward for you, but it was a huge help.'

'No problem.'

The other call was from Francis in KI's New York office.

'We have the handwriting analysis results on the postcard you gave me.'

'And?'

'Ninety-nine percent, it's the boss's handwriting. That is, Jack Kite.'

Luke said nothing. He tried to take this information in.

'Is there anything else you want me to do?' Francis asked.

'Yes,' Luke said. 'Look into flights from London to Athens.'

The call ended. Luke left the check-in queue. It might be possible to go straight from NYC. Luke asked at the desk. There were no imminent flights and the journey took fourteen hours, time he couldn't afford to waste at the moment. It would be almost as quick to get there via London.

He boarded his flight, too wired to sleep. He thought about Megan. Since talking to Mike, and then to Ian, a half-formed question had nagged at him. Now it articulated itself and forced him to think it through.

What if Megan knew what KI were up to in Burma before her birthday? If so, could she have planned the kidnap as a way to make KI do the right thing?

116

What if she'd suckered him, by making him a partner just before the kidnap? If that was her game, Luke wasn't sure whether to be proud of Megan or angry with her. She had taken charge of KI, after all. Surely she could have stopped what they were up to without terrifying Luke and her friends?

Mike had given Luke a sense of how sensitive and complex the Burma situation was. When it came down to it, a bunch of corrupt crooks were running a country and KI had to stop helping them. Tomorrow, Luke would weigh in. Before he went to Athens, it was time for him to tackle Stella Lock.

Twenty-Three

KITE INDUSTRIES HQ, SOHO, LONDON

Kite Industries' Chief Executive was an immaculately preserved brunette in a sombre suit and white blouse. She wore no jewellery but for a wedding ring. She looked forty-five at most, but Ian knew from his research that she was nearly fifty.

'How many copies of this video are there?' he asked at their 7 a.m. meeting.

'Ethan Thompson made three copies. One for you. One for us. One for Luke, when he returns from the US.'

'Luke is still in the air at the moment,' Ian told Stella. 'I'll have it couriered over once he's arrived.'

'I hope he got some useful information out of his father.'

Ian nodded. He didn't trust Stella enough to tell her about Luke's paternity. Or that Luke had already emailed him the information Mike Kite had given him. Ian was having this information analyzed at Special Branch.

'Let's watch the last part again,' he said.

Stella scanned the recording backwards.

'One more thing,' the pale Megan said. 'I understand that there has been a news blackout surrounding my kidnap, doubtless for good reasons. But if KI have not met the BMFF's conditions by midday on Sunday, UK time, then this video will be released to the media. KI will have to explain why they have kept my kidnapping secret for so long, and they will have to justify their abhorrent behaviour in Burma, which breaks international law. This will make KI the target of protestors all over the world, and should lead to bad publicity and boycotts, all of which I support. So I urge Stella Lock and the KI board: do the right thing. Withdraw from Burma. Now!'

The recording cut.

'Do you think she's suffering from Stockholm Syndrome?' Stella asked Ian.

Ian had yet to see a trace of emotion in Stella, but there was compassion in her voice. 'Twenty-seven percent of kidnap victims do, according to the FBI,' he told her. 'I think Megan supports the kidnappers to some extent. At the very least, she agrees that KI should withdraw from Burma. Non-cooperation with the military junta is also the British government's position.'

'But British weapons still find their way to Burma.'

'Some,' Ian said. 'Not many.'

'Do you think they'll hurt Megan if we don't comply?'

'Not in the short term. If you make a token gesture, begin the process of withdrawing all workers from the country, then I doubt she'll come to harm. If you act quickly, they might not send out the video recording.'

Stella shook her head. 'We'd be giving in to kidnappers.'

'As other companies do all the time. I'm sure you're nothing if not pragmatic.'

Stella looked aggrieved. 'We don't have all the information necessary to withdraw everyone in Burma. I'm still trying—'

Ian interrupted and played his trump card. 'Mike Kite is cooperating to help his niece. He's given Luke Kite a series of codes, names and addresses. Soon I'll be in a position to identify all aspects of KI's Burma operation. Then you'll be able to close everything down.'

Stella shook her head. 'If we close the Burma operation down completely, it will badly damage our reputation in the region. It may put some of our people at risk of arrest.'

'It's a chance that you have to take. Contract a private plane. Fly everyone home tomorrow night. Announce it at a press conference on Saturday. Megan will be freed and KI will get some good publicity.'

'If we do that, KI will become known as the softest touch in the entire Western hemisphere.'

Ian was irritated. This wasn't how he had expected this meeting to go. 'Do you have a better idea?'

'Yes,' Stella said. 'As a matter of fact, I do.'

Twenty-Four

Since making the video, Megan only slept in her cell at night. The room they let her use in the day had its windows taped over, so she couldn't see where she was, but it also had a comfortable sofa, a TV and DVD player. There was no TV reception, though, so she couldn't watch her soaps or the news.

She could watch DVDs about Burma. Yesterday she'd seen a film called *Beyond Rangoon*. Then she watched a documentary about the protest movement, *Burma VJ: Reporting from a Closed Country*. It had been nominated for an Oscar, for all the difference that made. Most of the people who made it, using hidden cameras, had been arrested or forced to flee Burma. The country remained closed, its citizen locked in, with little freedom. Just like her, she couldn't help but note.

This morning she'd watched a short film, *Orphans of the Storm*, set shortly after the earlier documentary. It told the story of thousands of children abandoned by the government after a typhoon destroyed their homes and killed their parents. When international aid was finally allowed in, most of it was stolen by corrupt officials. The film made her cry. Last, she was shown footage of the dictator's daughter's wedding. Millions of dollars spent on jewellery alone.

If there was a more evil government in the world, Megan didn't know about it. How could her company be dealing with the military dictatorship? Uncle Mike had few morals, but she was still surprised to see him stoop so low.

Henry joined her. 'You've been crying.'

She nodded. 'Those poor kids. That six-year-old girl, with her sad eyes, desperate for a few grains of rice. I just wanted to go over there, scoop them up, adopt them or something.'

'I know what you mean.' He put his arms around her. She buried her head in his chest. It made her think of Ethan. When she lifted her head, Henry tried to kiss her. She pulled away.

'Don't . . . I have a boyfriend.'

'Sorry,' Henry said. 'What we're doing, it's very lonely work.'

'But you're here by choice,' Megan reminded him.

'I thought you were on our side.'

'I am now,' she said, convincingly, 'but locking someone up, using a false name, making them incredibly vulnerable, then trying to kiss them – never a good romantic technique.'

Henry gave a wry smile. 'When all this is over, which should be less than twenty-four hours, I hope we can be friends, meet on equal terms.'

'I'd like that,' Megan said, sounding like she meant it. 'Do you think they're really going to meet your . . . our demands?'

'It's all gone quiet, but we have a source who should be able to keep us in the loop with what's going down today.'

'You've got a mole in KI?'

'We have a contact close to the situation, put it that way.'

'Someone I know?' Megan had had her suspicions since the conversation she'd overheard, but kept them to herself.

Henry grinned. 'You won't get any more out of me. Here.' He produced a Hollywood romance DVD. 'Thought you might want to watch something light to help you unwind.'

'That'd be great, thanks.'

'Afraid I can't stay and watch it with you. We have some complicated arrangements to make . . .'

'No worries.' Megan put the film on but couldn't concentrate. She kept thinking. Henry/Phil had just confirmed two things: one, that he was a creepy guy, willing to exploit her vulnerability; two, that the kidnappers had a spy in her circle.

Who was it?

ISLINGTON, LONDON

'Are you less worried now?' Panya asked Ethan. She was visiting him to find out how he'd done in the meeting she set up.

'I guess. KI still haven't said that they'll meet the kidnappers' demands.'

'I'm sure they will.'

'There's a lot of money at stake. Never underestimate the greed of multinational corporations.'

'Did you learn that from Megan?' Panya asked.

'Megan's not greedy. She's been rich all her life and she's

used to money. It doesn't impress her. I wish that all the kidnappers wanted was a huge ransom.'

'Like it or not,' Panya said, 'Megan is partly responsible for what's going on in Burma.'

'How can that be? She only got control of the company last week.'

'According to the guy I set you up with, Megan was sent a bunch of literature and a letter about it weeks ago.'

'I see,' Ethan raged. 'They sent her a flyer in the mail and because she didn't immediately do everything she possibly could to deal with the world's injustice, she had to be kidnapped. Is that it?'

'I'm telling you what they think, not how I think.'

'I know. I'm sorry, I'm sorry.'

Ethan sat on the leather sofa with his head in his hands. Earlier, he had spoken at length to Ian Trevelyan, told him everything he could remember about the meeting with the BMFF activists, in the hope that it would give Special Branch some kind of lead on tracking down the kidnappers. At his request, Special Branch hadn't questioned Panya herself. He'd convinced them that she'd already told everything. Only she'd just let slip something that was new to him. The thing in the mail. Did she know more than she had already said?

'It's out of your hands now,' Panya told Ethan. 'The BMFF have given KI until Sunday. Let Special Branch and KI do their stuff. They'll reach some kind of a deal with the kidnappers very soon, I'm sure.'

BARBICAN, LONDON

'You're back!' Flick's voice from the bedroom.

'You're still here!' Luke charged through the apartment. His flight had been delayed and it had taken an age to get through Customs. It was nearly ten.

Flick was wearing one of his old T-shirts with logos from the fourth Led Zeppelin album. They kissed and cuddled and talked about how much they'd missed each other.

'Have the police been here?' Luke asked.

'No, but some people from KI security searched the place. They took away a load of Megan's mail. Was that OK?'

'Do you remember any stuff about Burma in there?'

'No. If I remembered anything about Burma I'd've mentioned it before, when we found out about the BMFF.'

'Sure. Only . . . did Megan ever talk about Burma, or Asian politics or anything like that?'

'Duh – we mainly talked about shopping and fashion and boys and TV and the net, the way normal people do.'

'OK. It was just a thought.'

The phone rang.

'Want me to get that?' Flick asked. 'I've taken a few messages for you.'

'No. I'll get it.'

Ethan Thompson was on the other end of the line.

'Have you seen the video?' he asked.

'What video?'

The buzzer went. Someone at the door.

'I think we need to talk,' Ethan said.

'Sure. Just give me time to shower and eat. Where?'

'Somewhere we won't be watched . . . or overheard.'

He was implying that this phone might be bugged. Luke thought for a moment then came up with a solution. A place that Megan had promised to take him to more than once.

'You know where I mean when I say Megan's favourite coffee bar?'

'I do. I'll see you there in about an hour.'

Flick returned from the door holding a jiffy bag.

'A courier just delivered this.'

Luke tore the seal and pulled out a DVD.

'We'd better watch this before we go out,' he told Flick.

SOHO, LONDON

Ethan took Panya with him to Bar Italia. Like him, she was about to start the university term (the second year, in her case, studying Law at University College). He wanted her there to help explain stuff to Luke. Today was Saturday. The deadline for KI to withdraw from Burma was midday tomorrow, twenty-five hours away. So far, there was no sign of KI doing so.

The place was crowded. Luke arrived five minutes late, wearing a designer leather jacket, with Flick on his arm.

'There's someone I want to introduce,' Ethan told the couple.

He explained who Panya was and how she had helped.

'You're not a member of the BMFF?' Luke asked her.

'No,' Panya told them. 'And I don't support their methods. But the situation in Burma is desperate. There are elections coming up and all sorts of horrible things are happening. So, if I'm honest, I do have some sympathy with what they're doing.'

'Listen,' Luke said, lowering his voice. 'Do you think it's at all possible that Megan has been planning this all along?'

Ethan couldn't believe what he was hearing. 'You think she allowed herself to get kidnapped in order to put pressure on KI to withdraw from Burma? Come on!'

'I didn't say it's what I think. But what do you think?' Luke asked Panya.

'How would I know?' Panya asked. 'I've never met your cousin. And the people I talked to would never share that kind of information with me, even if it were true.'

'You and Grace know her best,' Luke told Ethan.

That was gracious of him, Ethan thought, albeit blindingly obvious. Luke had spent less than a month in his cousin's company, total, his whole life.

'I don't think that Megan would pull a stunt like that,' he told Luke. 'She's always straight with everyone.'

'I agree. I plan to insist on seeing Stella Lock today, ask what KI is doing. I'll tell her to withdraw all of KI's people from Burma. That's if she wants to keep her job.'

'How can you boss her around?' Ethan asked. 'Megan owns the company. With her out of the way, Stella Lock's in complete control.'

'Actually,' Luke said. 'It's no longer as simple as that.'

KITE INDUSTRIES HQ, LONDON

'I'm sorry,' Luke explained to Flick, leaving her outside the building. 'They won't let me bring anyone else in.'

'Where should I wait for you?' his girlfriend wanted to know.

'After this, I need to meet Ian. It may be best to call you later, when I know what's going on.'

'I'm sorry to sound clingy, it's just that you've only been back a couple of hours and—'

'I know, I know. I wish we could . . . you know. But I really have to do this, straight away.'

She gave him a long, lingering kiss, then let him go inside.

'Mr Kite?' The security guard practically saluted. A sharp contrast with his last visit to KI UK. 'Ms Lock is expecting you.'

Luke took the private elevator up to the fifth floor. The door opened into Stella Lock's office, which used to be his father's. An elegant, well-dressed woman stood when he entered the room. She held out her hand.

'Luke! We meet at last.'

Twenty-Five

BLOOMSBURY, LONDON

'What did you think of Luke?' Ethan asked Panya.

Ethan was fuming about Megan signing over half the company to him; he wasn't even sure if he believed it.

'I thought he was cute. I can see why Flick likes him.'

'I meant, as a person.'

'Quite serious, but it's a serious situation he's in.'

'Did you trust him?'

'Hold on.' They were in the student flat she shared with two other girls on her course. She had invited him back for lunch. Panya served fried haloumi with a green salad.

'I only met him for twenty-five minutes, Eef. It takes months before you decide to trust someone. And even then . . .'

She gave him a look like he had broken her trust, which he didn't think was fair. He'd hurt her, OK, but he hadn't meant to. He liked her as much now as he had when they were going out. He felt guilty about that and it was confusing him.

'I don't trust Luke,' he told Panya. 'And I don't understand why Megan decided to give him half the company.'

'I think you're hacked off she did it without telling you.'

'Maybe there's a little bit of that in it, too,' Ethan admitted. He'd forgotten how well Panya could read him.

'Were you hoping she'd share it all with you?' Panya asked.

That was a thought Ethan hadn't allowed himself to think. He didn't think about it now.

'I hope he'll phone,' he said, 'let me know if KI are going to do what the BMFF want.'

'You could phone him.'

'He's probably still in a meeting with Stella Lock,' Ethan said, but tried Luke's mobile anyway. It went straight to voicemail. He tried the Barbican flat. The same. He left a message: 'Call me when you get this.'

'He's probably having a good time with Flick and has forgotten all about keeping you in the loop,' Panya said.

'I don't see how he can have a good time when Megan's in such danger.'

Panya put down her fork. She began to massage his neck. She was always good at making him relax.

'Luke's sixteen. Flick might be his first girlfriend. He's done everything he can to help Megan. And don't forget, she's only his cousin. He doesn't even know her well. It's hardly surprising if he turns his phone off and goes to ground with Flick. If there's any news, I'm sure he'll call you. If you like, I can call some of the *Free Burma Now!* people I saw before, see if I can find out more about what the BMFF are up to.'

'That's be good. But don't put yourself in danger.'

KITE INDUSTRIES HQ, LONDON

They kept going over the rescue plan.

'It looks risky,' Luke told Stella Lock.

'Not to act would be even more risky. Think about it, Luke. Let's say we withdraw from Burma. We decommission as much of our technology as we can and bring everyone home tomorrow morning. There's still no guarantee that the BMFF will free Megan. Indeed, they might up their demands, hurt Megan and make us look extremely weak and foolish.'

'That's an acceptable risk. What you're proposing isn't.'

'And say we do get Megan back, safe and sound? Other pressure groups or terrorist organizations will see how easily we capitulated to kidnappers, making you and your cousin even more at risk in future. You'll have to travel with heavily-armed guards at all times. Do you want that?'

'No, but there's been a news blackout. Nobody would know except the BMFF.'

'You don't think that all these far-left groups are affiliated with each other?'

'I don't know anything,' Luke admitted. 'In the USA, people who act like this tend to be right-wing nut-jobs.'

'Recently, perhaps, but your country had plenty of dangerous, violent, left-wing protest groups in the sixties and seventies.'

Luke wasn't interested in ancient history. He was interested in tonight.

'In the attack you're planning, Megan could get hurt.'

'That's not very likely. Let me go over it with you again.'

'I suppose . . .' Earlier in their meeting, Stella had made it clear that, in Megan's absence, she had complete control over KI. Legally, until he was eighteen, Luke's role was non-existent. At best it was a *courtesy* role, as Stella put it. He could advise and comment, but he was there to learn, not make decisions. Luke knew better than to argue. To have any real influence, he needed Megan back.

'You're sure this is where they're holding Megan?'

'Ninety percent. We've been keeping a close watch on a BMFF member, Panya Morten. She's an ex-girlfriend of the Thompson boy. That's how we think they got the information about the eighteenth party she was taken from. Have you met her?'

'Once. She seemed all right to me.'

'Of course she did. I'm sure she told you that she was a mild, peaceful supporter of democratic rights in Burma. But she's a jilted lover with dangerous connections. We followed the people she talked to earlier in the week and have used every means available to work out where they're holding Megan.'

'Before acting, shouldn't we involve Special Branch?'

'We'll inform them and the police of what we're doing. They won't interfere. But speed is of the essence. You agree?'

'Yes, of course.'

'Then, please back me up when you talk to Ian Trevelyan. We raid the BMFF tonight, just after dark.'

Half an hour later, Luke was with Ian Trevelyan at New Scotland Yard.

'I'm not happy,' Luke said. 'There's some risk to Megan. But Stella wouldn't consider doing what the kidnappers ask.'

'What KI are proposing is extreme,' Ian told him. 'But it may offer the best solution to the situation.'

'I thought KI withdrawing from Burma offered the best solution.'

'I'd like KI to get out of Burma, too, but nobody wants to be seen to give in to terrorist threats. It creates a terrible precedent.'

Luke hated having so little control. He felt cornered. 'You think we have to go with it?'

'I think we do, yes. I've been talking to my superiors and they've just authorized me to make this a joint operation.'

'Stella says that I can join her in the KI security control room tonight. Do you think I should be there?'

'Up to you. But you mustn't go anywhere near the scene of the attack.'

'She wouldn't even tell me where it is.'

Twenty-Six

The kidnappers were getting jumpy. That made Megan feel jumpy. The deadline was sixteen hours away. If the video she'd made was released to the media, it would do great damage to KI's reputation. Megan would prefer that not to happen. It was the family name, the family business.

Henry joined her in the TV room.

'Time to move you back to the cell. For the last time, I hope.'

'Any news?'

'Can't tell you that,' he said, with the smallest shake of the head. 'Let's go.'

They were at the door when he got a call on his mobile.

'Wait there,' he said, pushing the door closed. Megan heard a heavy rumbling outside the building. She heard Henry saying, 'I see' and, 'When?' Then he returned.

'Quickly!' Henry said.

'What's happening? Are we in danger?'

'I don't know for sure. Nobody outside the organization knows we're in this building and nobody else has a reason to come here. This area's been marked for redevelopment since . . .'

There was a crashing noise. The whole building shook.

From elsewhere in the building. Megan could hear shouting. *We're under attack*. Henry swore.

'This way!' They charged down the metal steps. They were heading down the route on which Megan had tried to escape before. This time, when they got to the bottom, instead of turning left, Henry grabbed Megan's hand and led her to the back of the building, kicking open a set of double fire doors. They ran into a big, dark, empty space.

'Is the van ready?' he shouted, but there was no reply.

Megan followed Henry. This would be the time to make a break for it, but he was gripping her hand and, anyway, clearly had her safety in mind. There was a series of loud bangs. Outside the building she could hear heavy footsteps, like an army on the march. Henry gripped her hand tighter.

'I don't know where the others are. We had a plan, but . . .'

Megan couldn't hear the rest because there was an explosion nearby. Behind them, the building began to shudder and strain. Then the shooting started.

KITE INDUSTRIES HQ, LONDON

Luke sat next to Stella Lock in front of a twelve-screen video console. Jim Pierce and a KI security team were with the police at a hide-out somewhere in North London. Luke didn't know where the hide-out was but he'd been told how they'd found it: by bugging Ethan's friend Panya and following her every move. A KI agent had tailed Panya to her meeting with a BMFF member, then followed the BMFF guy to the hide-out.

That morning, Luke had promised Ethan he'd call when he knew what was going on. A promise he was unable to keep.

'Something's happening,' Stella Lock said. She was wearing headphones and had a mike suspended in front of her mouth. Luke didn't like that she could hear things he couldn't. On the screen in front of him, a flare went up. Or maybe it was a bomb going off.

'Are we attacking them?' Luke asked. 'Isn't there a risk that Megan will be hurt?'

'It's probably a diversion,' Stella explained. 'Not a real bomb. The idea is to make them think the trouble is in one area so that they escape through another, straight into our arms.'

'Sounds like a plan.' Luke noticed concern spread across her face. 'What's wrong?'

'I thought I heard gunshots. We didn't think the kidnappers were armed. Maybe it's only our lot, going in.' She pressed a button. 'Jim? Jim, can you hear me?'

There was a pause. Then, 'I see,' she said. 'OK. I'll wait.'

She turned to Luke. 'The gunshots were from our side. They thought they were under attack.'

'But they weren't?' Luke asked.

'I don't know. One feels rather . . . impotent here in this control room, doesn't one?'

Luke had never heard anyone use 'one' that way before. It was too English for him, show-off creepy. He turned to Miles, the guy in charge of the technical surveillance operation. 'Is there any way that I can hear what's going on, too?'

Miles looked at Stella.

'You can tune him in to the outside microphone,' she said.

She wasn't going to let Luke hear what Jim Pierce said, but at least he would have a better feel for what the situation was like on the ground. Miles handed him a set of headphones.

'How long have we been listening to the kidnappers?' Luke asked.

'Just over a day.'

They'd known where she was for a day and left her there. Luke put the headphones in. He heard rapid footsteps. He heard distant shouting. He heard a rumbling noise. Then he heard another explosion, a big one. He looked at the screen. The biggest of the warehouse buildings, the one where KI thought that the BMFF were holding Megan, was on fire. Large parts of it were falling to the ground. Suddenly, in perfect sync, three ancient sets of windows exploded outwards.

'This is not going according to plan,' Stella Lock said.

ISLINGTON, LONDON

Ethan kept calling Luke but his mobile went to voicemail every time. Panya hadn't called him back either. Ethan was using her; he was aware of that. Sometimes, he'd learned, you had no choice but to use people. Including those you cared about.

Mum was getting ready to go out to dinner.

'You look on edge,' she said.

'Have you heard anything?' he asked. 'Anything at all?'

'Last time I spoke to the Home Secretary, he seemed confident that the whole affair would get sorted out by the deadline tomorrow. Don't worry. Kite Industries won't risk losing Megan in order to appease a military dictatorship. She'll be all right.'

She kissed him on the forehead. 'I'm meeting friends in twenty minutes. But I'll cancel if you don't want to be alone.'

'It's OK. Like you said, there's nothing you can do. Grace is upstairs. She'll keep me company.'

His sister was almost as worried as he was. As soon as Mum was gone, Ethan went up to her room.

'Any news?'

'Not a word.'

'Have you called Panya?'

'I can't.' Ethan explained why.

'I hate not being in the loop,' Grace said.

'Me too.'

'Some days,' she confessed, 'I wish I'd never teamed up with Megan.'

'You can't say that!'

'I can say it because of how much I care about her. You weren't there for her all those times, Eef. Her mum dying. She'd only just got over that when her dad died. Then there was the nightmare that followed that. I'm forced to think about it every time I try to walk more than a few steps. Now this. I love her like a sister and I'd never let her down, but if I think back to that first day of school, when I chose to sit next to her . . . it's just, knowing what I know now . . . sometimes I think her whole family must be cursed.'

'That's baby talk,' Ethan told her. 'It'll be OK. We'll stick with her. It'll be OK.'

Grace burst into tears and rested her head on his shoulders.

'I wish I could believe you,' she said.

Ethan wished he could believe himself.

Twenty-Seven

THE BARBICAN, LONDON

Flick was waiting for Luke when he got back to the apartment.

'What happened?' she asked. 'Is Megan free?'

Luke shook his head. 'I don't know. There was gunfire. There was an explosion. People may have been killed.'

'That's terrible!' Flick looked very upset. Luke felt numb. He was still trying to take it all in.

'The kidnappers and Megan were holed up in an area full of abandoned warehouses, waiting to be developed. One of the warehouses caught fire. It burned so badly that the police couldn't get near it. Some of the BMFF people got away. At least, a van left a nearby building while the raid was going on, but that could have been coincidence. They're going to search the burned-out warehouse for remains tomorrow, but it's bound to take a long time to identify the dead.'

'Oh, Luke. That's so, so awful.'

Tears poured down her cheeks. They hugged each other. He looked at the time. It was late, but he knew Ethan would want to be woken. He couldn't tell him that KI thought Panya was working both sides and they had been spying on her. Panya probably knew what had happened already, but he doubted she would have told Ethan. He made the call.

'It's bad news, I'm afraid.'

Five minutes later, when he put the phone down, all he could do was flop onto the sofa with Flick.

'I don't believe Megan's dead,' Flick said.

'I hope you're right.'

'Do you know where they were holding her?'

'I wasn't meant to know, but the fire was on the radio news when I was coming home. North London, a wasteland area that's waiting to be built on.'

'I think we should go there when it's light, take a look.'

'You're right. I need to see where it happened.'

'What are Kite Industries going to do about the deadline?'

'I don't know.'

'If the BMFF send the video to the media tomorrow, won't that mean that Megan is still alive?'

'I don't know.'

They both went to bed, but Luke couldn't drift off. Two possible scenarios haunted him. One: KI had deliberately murdered both the kidnappers and Megan tonight, knowing that this was the easiest way to get rid of the Burma bad publicity problem. No, he couldn't accept that Megan was dead. Not until it was confirmed. Which left scenario two: Megan was still playing them. She hadn't been killed, but had forced KI to show their hand, giving her extra leverage to make them withdraw from Burma. Both scenarios were so cynical that Luke found them hard to credit. He turned over all of the last week's events in his mind, coming to no conclusions whatsoever.

BLOOMSBURY, LONDON

Ethan walked from Islington to Panya's place in Bloomsbury. The walk took the best part of an hour in the autumn drizzle. He had time to think. According to Luke, last night's raid had been a disaster. Megan might be dead.

The rain hid his tears from passers-by.

It was nearly midday, the hour that Megan's video about Burma should be sent to the media. Then, all hell would break loose. Ethan didn't want to be home. Enough people knew about his relationship with Megan for the media to camp out on his door. Better to be with someone he trusted.

His phone rang. Mum.

'Have you heard anything?' he asked.

'Nothing,' Mum replied. 'I wondered if you'd seen your friend yet, whether she has any news.'

'I'm nearly at her door. I decided to walk.'

'Call us if she has any news at all, will you? Your sister's very, very upset.'

'I will.' Ethan hung up. He looked at the headlines on the news-stand at Russell Square tube station. Nothing about last night's conflagration, which had taken place far too late for the Sunday papers. Nothing about Burma, or KI. He looked at his watch. Five to twelve. All that was about to change.

He rang Panya's buzzer and she let him in. She was still in her kimono-style dressing gown. From the look of her, she'd slept as badly as he had.

'Are you alone?'

'The others are back with their families for the weekend.'

'Could you put on the midday news?'

'Uh. Sure.' She turned on the TV, then went for a wash. Nothing about the kidnapping, or a video.

'I guess the midday deadline doesn't mean they'll send out the DVD that instant,' Ethan said when Panya returned. 'Have you heard anything, anything at all?'

Panya nodded.

'What?'

'It's not good,' she said.

NORTH LONDON

Yellow police tape sealed the affected area. Luke and Flick were still able to get a good view of the situation. Two huge warehouses had collapsed. In places, the debris rose higher than a double-decker bus. At the edges of the site, mechanical digging and heavy-lifting equipment were already in place. It was obvious that excavating the wreckage would take days, if not weeks. The chances of anyone inside having survived was minimal, even Luke could see that.

'You said a van got away?' Flick asked.

'KI thinks so, but they're not sure. I saw something on screen. That's not to say that Megan was in it.'

Jim Pierce, wearing an orange protective jumpsuit, charged up to the couple.

'What are you doing here?'

'We're taking a look, that's all. It isn't dangerous, is it?'

'Not from this distance, no,' Pierce admitted. 'But I don't want you out in public.'

'What do you mean?'

'You're at risk of being kidnapped yourself.'

'Bull. People don't even know that . . .' Luke stopped himself. He was sometimes in danger of forgetting what people knew about him. That he was really Megan's brother, not cousin – he hadn't even told Flick that, only Ian and Celine knew. Then there was his owning half of KI – the same people plus Flick and the Thompsons knew about that. And Stella Lock. And if she knew, probably Pierce knew too.

' "People don't even know" what?' Pierce asked, impatient.

'Never mind. Have the kidnappers delivered the video to the media yet?'

Pierce shook his head. 'With luck, the video's buried with the kidnappers, somewhere over there.'

'But if the kidnappers were killed, that means . . .'

Before Luke could formulate the thought, Pierce snapped at him. 'Get out of here, Luke. If you won't let me give you bodyguards, see your Special Branch friend, get into protective custody.'

'Let's go,' Flick said.

They left the site. 'I won't hide,' Luke told Flick.

'Maybe you ought to,' Flick told him. 'Didn't you say that someone tried to grab you in Nice? Maybe that was the BMFF. Still, I find it hard to believe they would have let Megan . . .'

Her voice trailed off.

Luke began to take in what had probably happened. KI had, by attacking the warehouses, assured Megan's death. And he, Luke, had agreed to it. He had been very, very stupid. It was time to reassess. It was time to mourn. But both Flick and Jim were right. He was in great danger.

It was time to go. But where?

Twenty-Eight

BLOOMSBURY, LONDON

At Ethan's insistence, Panya made a couple of phone calls to confirm her suspicions. Both calls were brief and brutal. She put the phone down.

'I don't know how to tell you this,' she said to Ethan.

He gripped the arm of the chair he was sitting in, but said nothing.

'Understand, I've not talked to anybody who was directly involved, but people who've talked to people who—'

'Just tell me,' Ethan snapped.

'The Kite Industries people attacked the warehouse where they were holding Megan with much more force than was necessary. The BMFF group are peaceful people, Eef, they don't use guns. But they did have some explosives planted in sensitive places. The idea was to create a diversion so that, in the case of an attack, they'd have time to get away. But the explosion ignited some gas canisters they didn't know about in an adjacent building. Two huge warehouses caught fire. The only people who got away were the guards who set off the diversionary explosion. Everyone else was trapped inside when the building went up.'

'Including Megan.'

'I'm afraid so.'

Ethan groaned, trying not to imagine the scene. Failing. A quick death would have been tragic, but more bearable. To know that she had suffered the fear, the heat . . .

'There, there.' Panya wiped his face. The tears were still streaming down. 'Come on now, I'll look after you.'

He buried his head in her chest.

THE BARBICAN, LONDON

When they got back to the apartment, Luke called Ian Trevelyan to talk things over.

'There's no evidence that anybody died last night,' Ian told him. 'Jim Pierce is scaremongering. If it was time to grieve for your sister, I would tell you, believe me. Don't. She's probably OK. Right now, it's yourself you need to worry about.'

He and Luke talked over Luke's options.

'Where will you go?' Flick asked when Luke came off the phone. 'Can I come too?'

'I don't know,' Luke said. 'I don't want to put you in danger. You know, someone was killed in the elevator outside this apartment. Even here, we're at risk.'

'Then get KI security to provide a permanent guard.'

'I don't trust them,' Luke said. 'For all I know . . .'

'What?'

Luke hesitated. He didn't want to share his most paranoid imaginings with Flick. On the other hand, he had to trust somebody. If not her, who?

'It's just possible that the explosion last night was caused by KI rather than by the kidnappers. They may have decided that it's better to have Megan out of the way than to have her doing what she wants in Burma.'

Flick's expression was sceptical. 'You'd better be incredibly careful, then. Where do you feel most secure?'

'Not here, that's for sure.'

And not with his mom in Greenwich Village. If he showed up back in New York, the police would hassle him again, wanting a lead on Mike. Luke was happiest and felt safest when he was staying with Andy in Brooklyn. Only Andy's mom had made it clear that he wasn't welcome there. His dad had a couple of other places that Luke knew about: one in Paris, another in Ireland. But he'd never been to either.

'Maybe we should run away together,' Flick said. 'We've both got those company credit cards.'

'Through which KI can keep tabs on wherever we are.'

'Not necessarily. I probably shouldn't be telling you this, but I set up an online payment account with mine . . .'

She showed him how she'd done this. It took a couple of minutes. Once he'd set up the account, Luke was able to order things over the net and pay using the online account, which instantly debited his company credit card. KI should have no way of hacking into the online account to see what he'd bought.

'We can get cash advances on the card here before we travel, then change it into whatever currency we like,' Flick said. 'So where shall we go?'

Was it wise to leave when all this was going on? Luke couldn't decide. He would, however, feel safer on the run than he would staying here. And there was something else he had to do. He hadn't told Flick about the postcard from Athens. Ian Trevelyan had suggested he keep that story strictly to himself.

'Have you ever been to Greece?' he asked her. 'I've always wanted to visit the Acropolis.'

BLOOMSBURY, LONDON

'I ought to go.' Ethan felt lousy. Megan might be dead but she wasn't gone. She was in his head. Hungover, remembering what he'd done the night before, he could feel her watching him. It was a terrible feeling.

'Have a shower first,' Panya said. 'You look like hell.'

'I'll have a bath when I get in.' Ethan checked his phone. Two messages from his sister. One missed call from Luke. He would deal with them later.

'Will you call me?'

'Of course.' He kissed her on the cheek and beat a rapid retreat.

On the street, it was turning cold. He thought about taking a tube, but he needed to think. He checked the messages from Grace. She'd heard nothing. He wasn't ready to tell her the worst. He called Luke.

'You just caught me,' he said. 'I'm leaving the country.'

'Why? We need to talk.'

'I'm meeting Flick in an hour, but I'm already packed.

Why don't we meet for coffee before that? Where are you?'

Ethan told him. They arranged to meet at a café just off the Tottenham Court Road.

Twenty minutes later, his girlfriend's cousin bought him a double espresso. Luke had a bag with him, a leather knapsack, small enough to take as hand luggage. He looked a lot better than Ethan felt. Losing his cousin couldn't have hit him all that hard, Ethan reckoned.

'Going home?'

'No. Somewhere else. I'm not safe here. Not after . . .'

Ethan understood. With Megan gone, Luke was an obvious target.

'Where then?'

'You're better off not knowing.'

'Are you taking Flick with you?'

'Yeah.' Luke looked doubtful. 'You think that's crazy?'

'I don't know. I can see you need company but . . .' Ethan could hardly criticize Luke for wanting to escape with his girlfriend. 'She could be a liability, that's all I'm saying.'

'A liability? I've heard Megan use that word. Does it have some kind of English double meaning? Flick's pretty sharp, you know. She helps me to keep on my toes.'

'I'm sorry. It's just that, after what's happened to Megan . . .'

'We don't know for sure what's happened to Megan,' Luke said. 'Does your mum know anything? She's a government minister, right?'

'Right. Only she deals with pensions, not security. She

hasn't heard a thing. Panya spoke to her friends who have friends in the BMFF. And . . .'

'And?'

Ethan didn't know how to put this, so he blurted it out. 'According to her, a couple of people got out, the ones who were guarding the entrance. Everyone else, including Megan, died in the explosion.'

Luke closed his eyes. Ethan thought that he was going to cry, but after a minute or so, he opened them again, seemed to collect himself, and stood up. He offered Ethan his hand.

'I don't know if I'll ever see you again, so I just wanted to say, you were kind to my sister and I appreciate that. I know you must be hurting as much as I am. Take care.'

Understandable, in the circumstances, that Luke should still think of Megan as his sister. Ethan shook his hand.

'You look after yourself too,' he said. 'If I can ever help, you know where to find me.'

Luke turned on to Tottenham Court Road. He stopped outside a currency exchange booth that stayed open late. Why there? Ethan wondered. Presumably so that the transaction wouldn't be traced. Ethan watched the youth get out his wallet.

A brown estate car braked abruptly in front of the booth, blocking Ethan's view. It looked wrong. You weren't allowed to park there.

Ethan ran across the road, swerving between a bus and a taxi. A big guy in dark shades and a black cap got out of the back seat of the brown car.

'Luke! Look out!'

Luke turned round. Another, even larger guy was getting

out of the estate car. His face was obscured by a baseball cap and dark, wrap-around glasses.

Luke ran out of the exchange booth. He shot down Tottenham Court Road. Ethan managed to place himself between the pursuers and the escaping lad.

'Looking for someone?' he asked the men in dark glasses.

The two men stood in front of him, snarls on their lips. For a moment, Ethan thought they were going to take him instead. Ethan would make a pretty good hostage. He was, after all, a government minister's son. But the two men couldn't know that. They glanced at each other, then got back into the car, which sped off. Ethan memorized the number.

'Was the guy who ran off a friend of yours?' called the young Asian man behind the currency exchange counter.

'Yes, why?'

The young man pointed. Luke had left his wallet behind. Ethan picked it up and got out his phone to call Luke. While he was waiting for Luke to answer, Flick arrived.

'You weren't who I was expecting to see,' she said. 'Has something happened?'

Ethan explained.

'The sooner we get out of here,' she said, 'the better.'

Luke answered his phone.

'Are they gone?' he asked.

'They've gone. I got their number.'

'You saved my ass, Eef. I owe you.'

Luke had never called him 'Eef' before.

'No problem.'

'Have you got Ian Trevelyan's number?' Luke asked him.

'Yes.'

'Call him. Give him the licence number of the car that tried to kidnap me.'

'I'll do that. Flick's here. I'll pass you over.'

He heard the girl say, 'Where are you?' and 'No worries, I'll change the money then get a cab and pick you up. OK, I'll tell him. Yes, your wallet's still here. I'll be five minutes.'

Ethan waited while she changed a lot of money into euros at a rather poor rate.

'I've got to go. We fly out in a couple of hours. Thanks for your help. If you see Megan before we do, give her our love.'

She kissed him on the cheek. Did Flick not realize that Megan was dead? When would Luke tell her? Not Ethan's problem.

There were two cabs coming down the road. Flick got into the first one. Ethan took the second, back to Islington, where he had to break the terrible news to Grace.

Twenty-Nine

HEATHROW AIRPORT, LONDON

Luke picked up a copy of the *Evening Standard* before they checked in for their flight. The warehouse fires the previous night got two paragraphs on page seven. *Police blamed the explosions on heating gas canisters that had not been properly disposed of. While there are no known casualties, a team is exploring the debris in case the warehouses were used by rough sleepers.* That was the final insult to his sister. If Megan's body was found, she would be assumed to be a down-and-out.

Once he was through the security checks, Luke felt more secure. Airports were a kind of limbo, where, no matter who might be after you, they could not smuggle weapons in, or smuggle a body out. He and Flick had half an hour to spare. He decided to ring Ian Trevelyan, the one adult he trusted. The Special Branch man answered on the second ring.

'Luke, I've spoken to Ethan Thompson. I gather you're on your travels?'

'Yes.'

'Don't tell me where you're going, just in case we're being listened in on.'

'OK, have you had time to trace the car that the people who attacked me were using?'

'Stolen, I'm afraid.'

Luke told him what Ethan had said about Megan dying. 'Have you found any bodies in last night's warehouse fire?'

'No. And if she really was dead, we would have done. Were you aware that KI's dirty squad were going to use explosives?'

'No. I thought that the explosives were all from the kidnappers' side?'

'The kidnappers' explosives were more like smoke bombs. It was the KI ones that ignited the gas canisters.'

This fitted with what he'd seen on the monitor screens.

'You think KI wanted Megan to die?'

'It's not beyond the bounds of possibility. Doesn't mean they succeeded. You're the one at risk now. Getting out of the country makes sense. Trust nobody.'

'There are only three people in the world I trust,' Luke said, 'and you're one of them.'

'Thanks for the vote of confidence. Whatever happens, Luke, keep your head down. Stay away from KI and everything to do with it. You may be its owner one day, but the company's a poisoned chalice. And stay in touch with me at all times.'

The call ended.

'What's wrong?' Flick asked.

'Nothing. Let's get on the plane, away from all this.'

ISLINGTON, LONDON

'He's *left the country*!' Ethan's sister was incredulous. 'Did you hear that, Mum?'

Florence Thompson put down her fork. Sunday dinner was the one time that the family always ate together. For the last few months, Megan had always been here too.

'Why shouldn't he leave the country?' Mum asked. 'Are you saying that Luke is suspect in all this?'

'Yes! If Megan really is dead, he inherits everything.'

'Only if he lives to be eighteen,' Ethan pointed out. 'Which is something that Megan nearly didn't manage. And Luke has twenty months to go.'

'Do you know where he is?' Mum asked.

Ethan shook his head. 'Flick was changing money into euros, so he can't have gone that far, but he said I was better off not knowing.'

'I suspect that we're all better off not knowing,' said Dad. 'The more that comes out about that boy's father, the more troubled I am.'

'You can't hold the sins of the father against the son,' Ethan said.

'Of course not, but Luke did visit Mike in prison this week. They're still close.'

'Really?' Ethan was shocked. 'Straight after the kidnap?'

'So I've been told,' Mum said. 'And don't think that Mike Kite is going to be in prison for ever. I hear the US authorities are having trouble building a case against him. Some witnesses seem to be having memory lapses, or changing their story.'

Ethan swore. He thought about Luke. How upset had the lad really been when Ethan told him that Megan was dead? He'd closed his eyes to hide his emotions. He might have been devastated, or he might have been thinking about all the money that was coming this way, and what he was going to get up to abroad with his sexy girlfriend.

'Megan trusted Luke,' Grace said. 'If she signed over half the company to him, that proves how much she trusted him.'

'It doesn't mean she was right,' Dad said. 'Megan could be impulsive and—'

'Don't speak ill of the dead,' Mum interrupted, and that shut everybody up. They finished their coq au vin in silence. Grace asked if she could turn on the early-evening news.

'Not while we're at the table,' Mum said.

'But I want to see if that video the BMFF made of Megan has been released to the media.'

'And what does it mean if it has?' Dad asked.

'That some of the people who took her survived the attack.'

'What would be the point of releasing the video after Megan's been killed?' Ethan asked. 'It would just make the BMFF look bad.'

'They haven't found Megan's body yet!' Grace protested. 'We can't be sure that she's . . . that she's . . .' She began to cry.

'Put the telly on,' Mum said.

They did. There was nothing about Megan, nothing about the warehouse fires, nothing about Burma. It was as if the last week hadn't happened at all, Ethan thought, like it had been a bad, irritating dream that woke you up. He wished it was.

'Isn't it about time we did something?' he asked his parents and sister. 'I mean, now that Megan's dead, why have a publicity blackout? Both the BMFF and Kite Industries messed up really badly. Shouldn't they both be exposed? Wouldn't Megan have wanted that?'

'Who are we to say what Megan would have wanted?' Grace asked.

Ethan had no answer. For the first time, it fully hit him that he would never speak to Megan again, never hear her silly laugh, or that bossy tone she used when she had to get her own way; the vulnerable, breathy late-night voice she only used with him, when they were alone; that excited, opinionated voice she had when she seized on an argument and they had it out. She could change her mind as easily as she made it up, if his ideas were strong enough. What would she want him to do? The right thing. But Ethan had no idea what that was.

Thirty

They had given her a knock-out shot, so Megan didn't know how long she'd been unconscious. Twenty-four hours, possibly much more. Her head was incredibly heavy and she felt sweaty, grubby, badly in need of a bath. So much for the extra freedom her captors promised for supporting them, for making the video. She had dreamed of being at sea, on a Caribbean cruise she'd been on years ago, when Mum was alive. They had pulled into an array of gorgeous islands, eaten endless fresh, exotic fruit.

What she wouldn't give for some fresh fruit now.

Megan got out of her single, metal bed, and banged the cell door with her fist. No response. The cell was similar to the makeshift one she'd been in before, but smelled different. And it was warmer. There was no sink, but at least she had a toilet.

Megan used the portaloo and drank warm water from a plastic bottle. There were energy bars to eat but she'd already had enough of those to last a lifetime. She could murder some fish and chips. Or even muesli, which she normally hated, as long as it came with fresh milk. And a mug of strong tea.

She had done everything they asked. And what had they

done? Drugged and dumped her. It wasn't fair. She had listened to all of their propaganda about Burma, agreed with everything they said, although it seemed one-sided to her. There are two sides to every story, Dad used to say. Some of what they told her about Burma had been familiar, though it took Megan days to remember where from. Then Henry mentioned that they had sent her a package of material about Burma a few weeks ago. When it arrived, Megan remembered, Flick, who always dealt with the junk mail, passed it to her, saying. 'Did you order this?'

Megan, as she recalled, had looked through the material, put it aside. She'd probably asked Flick to throw it out. Or maybe she'd hung onto it in case there was a reason she'd been sent it that she didn't know about yet.

Now she knew what the real reason was. Her kidnappers weren't trying to indoctrinate her in advance. They were trying to cover themselves. They wanted to show that Megan knew about the situation in Burma and did nothing about it. Only KI's involvement in Burma was secret. Megan hadn't known what the company were up to. Even now, she only had the kidnappers' word for it. Nevertheless she had made their video, backing up the claim. She had agreed to join the BMFF.

The video. Shouldn't that have been released by now? The deadline on the video was midday on Sunday. The kidnappers had moved her, in a panic, on what she assumed was a Saturday night. Megan's memories of the move were fuzzy, because of what happened during it. Fire. Explosions. Running downstairs, into the dark. Henry hustling her to safety, into the back of a van. The van setting off at speed.

Clinging on to Henry, bouncing about in the back. When the van stopped at lights, he apologized, then gave her the shot. When she woke, she was alone, and had been alone ever since.

Megan banged on the door again. There was nothing else she could think of to do.

ATHENS, GREECE

Flick was in raptures about Athens.

'I came in August once. It was baking and crowded and polluted, horrible. But this is lovely.'

Luke liked the way she said 'lovely'. So English. Athens was a lot warmer and dryer than London and the Byron hotel couldn't be better located. It was at the side of the Acropolis and only a short walk from the Plaka, on the north side of the Acropolis, where late-season tourists loitered in restaurants and bars. He and Flick were just in time to get a meal.

Flick insisted on ordering Retsina with her souvlaki. Luke sipped a little of the resiny wine, which came in a pink tin jug. They talked about visiting islands and museums. Flick reckoned that, if you wanted a good beach, you were better off on an island.

'Who did you come with before?' he asked her.

'My parents, not a boy if that's what you were thinking. Are you the jealous type?'

Luke shook his head. He had no idea what 'type' he was. Flick knew that she was his first girlfriend, but he hadn't the confidence to ask about the guys she'd been with before. When she tried to pour him more of the wine, he refused. She finished the jug, and was a little tipsy on the walk back to the hotel. She tripped over a low bollard and he had to catch her. When he'd helped her to stand up straight, she kissed him full on the lips.

'Luke Kite, my knight in shining armour. Why are we here, Luke?'

'What do you mean, *why*? To escape. To see the Acropolis. You said you fancied it, too.'

'I did. I do. But I wondered why you fancied it, and why we're staying in a cheap hotel, rather than a five star.'

'A five-star is the first place that people would look for me.'

'So is the Plaka. We could go to a much less popular part of town, or disappear completely in any of a hundred islands. But when I mentioned going to an island earlier, you blanked me. What was that about?'

It was because Luke wanted to stay at the Byron hotel until he had found Celine and/or his father. Failing that, he had to work out why a postcard in his father's handwriting had been sent from the Byron only a fortnight ago. But Luke didn't want to burden Flick with that information, which she might find scary. Especially not tonight. He waited for Flick to get distracted and, sure enough, she did.

'God, look at that view. Isn't it sensational?'

He agreed that it was and everything was all right. Tonight, he was on holiday.

Thirty-One

'What's going on?' Megan asked her new jailer. 'Where's Henry?'

'We have a security alert,' said the small man, who was wearing a ski mask. She couldn't place his accent but it didn't sound like he was born in the UK. 'You are safest here, in your room.'

'Is the deadline coming up?'

'I am not allowed to discuss such things with you.'

'I thought we were on the same side.'

The small man didn't reply. The ski mask meant that she had no opportunity to read the expression on his face. Warm air blew in from outside the container. Her captor put a tray on the floor, together with a newspaper, a copy of the *Financial Times*, dated Saturday. Was it only Saturday? Megan had no real idea. She'd thought it was Saturday on the day that they left her previous prison. That would mean she had only been gone for six days, whereas it felt like more than a week. If it was only six days, the deadline she'd given in the video hadn't expired yet.

'Henry said you were allowed to read the paper and apologizes for his absence. I will return later.'

'How about a shower? I could really use a shower.'

'Not today.'

When he had gone, Megan drank cheap apple juice and forced down a stale cheese sandwich. The quality of the food in this hotel was, if anything, getting worse. She picked up the paper. She would have preferred a radio, or the internet, but anything was better than nothing. She checked the price of KI stock: still rising. Nothing about her kidnapping, of course. But there was a mention that a date for the long delayed elections in Burma was about to be announced. Her kidnappers seemed to have their timing spot on.

ATHENS, GREECE

Flick wanted a lie-in. Luke said he'd see her downstairs. A woman served him breakfast on the ground floor of the small hotel. He showed her a photo of Dad.

'Have you seen this guy? Perhaps he stayed here?'

'No. I'm sorry. I have not been here long.'

Breakfast consisted of juice, coffee and a bread roll. Just enough to keep him going. Luke noted that there was a single laptop connected to the internet for the use of guests. A lad not much younger than him had been on it since he came down.

'Could I borrow that for five minutes?' Luke asked, when he'd finished his breakfast. The youth gave him a resentful look, then his eyes widened. Luke turned round to see Flick getting out of the lift. She wore a T-shirt and shorts.

'I'm just asking if I can borrow this computer,' Luke told her.

'So I see. We just need to check one teeny thing,' she explained to the guy, using her biggest, most innocent smile. The lad looked from Flick to Luke, as if to say, *How did you land a girl like that?* Then he said, 'Sure', and got out of the way.

'Did you order me breakfast?' Flick asked.

'No, I didn't know how long you'd be. They bring everyone the same thing anyway. The coffee's good.'

He checked a couple of news sites. Nothing about his sister, or KI's involvement in Burma. Then, on a whim, he went on Google Images and typed in *Celine Michel*.

The computer was slow, but dozens of faces gradually materialized. Celine's was a common name, it appeared, and there wasn't one woman who dominated. At first glance, none of the pictures looked like his father's girlfriend. There was an attractive black woman and a cute French-Canadian in a short skirt, both on Facebook, a photographer in Southern France, a female jockey, and a woman who ran a dance class in Melbourne, Australia. He clicked on the second page of entries, and there, in third position, was the woman he wanted, pictured at a conference of some kind with two other women. Celine Michel, designer. Her hair was a little longer than when he met her last week, and she was thinner, obviously, but she looked happy and pretty, with a champagne glass in her hand.

Flick's breakfast arrived. Luke beckoned the waitress over on her way back to the kitchen.

'Excuse me, do you know this woman?' he asked, his voice low enough for Flick not to hear.

'Yes, she is staying here. Mrs Jackson.'

'She's . . . ?' Luke tried not to show that this was a shock. He forced a smile. 'Thank you. We're friends. Would you happen to know her room number?'

'I'm sorry, no.'

There was nobody behind the reception desk for Luke to ask. He thought of sneaking a look at the register, but everything was on computer and he had trouble with the Greek alphabet, so all he was likely to do was look suspicious. He joined Flick, giving a wave to the young English lad who was gawping at her from a distance.

'All yours again, thanks.'

'Did you find anything you wanted to know?' Flick asked.

'Maybe.' He wasn't going to lie to his girlfriend, but she thought they were on holiday. He would leave telling her about Celine Michel until after they'd explored the Acropolis.

Four hours later, they walked back down the steep hill from the awesome, ancient temple. Luke thought it was the most impressive site he'd ever seen. If he didn't have more urgent things on his mind, he would like to investigate Greek history, the beginnings of democracy, all that stuff.

It was autumn, but Luke was baked in sweat, and couldn't imagine doing this climb in the height of summer. Flick began to talk about the new Acropolis museum and how it had spaces saved in it for the Parthenon marbles that some British lord had bought at a giveaway price centuries ago.

'That's the sort of thing Uncle Mike would have got up to. Where are these marbles now?' Luke asked.

'In the British Museum. Haven't you seen them?'

'Never been there, no. Tell you what, let's skip the museum and visit the marbles when we're back in London.'

'But we're here, now!'

'Yeah but . . . there's someone I want to catch at the hotel. I don't know how much longer she'll be staying here.'

'What?' Flick looked affronted, but not too affronted. 'I *knew* there had to be an ulterior motive for us coming here. Who is it, your mother?'

'No. Celine Michel.'

'The one whose flat you were nearly kidnapped outside in Nice? After which you left me on my own while you flew home?'

She had a right to be hacked off. 'That one, yes.'

'Why? Why have you followed her here?'

'It's not her I'm looking for. I'm after the person she's looking for.'

Flick frowned. 'And that person is . . . ?'

'*My father.*'

'But he's . . .'

'Not according to Celine.' Luke didn't mention the postcard that had reopened his doubts about whether Dad was dead. He'd already given Flick a lot of information to take in. There was an even more important bit to come.

'I'd like to meet this woman,' Flick said. 'Make her explain herself. OK, let's skip the museum.'

'There's one other thing I haven't told you about her,' Luke said.

'And what would that be?'

'She's pregnant. With *my dad's* child.'

Thirty-Two

'Where's Henry?'

'Henry's not here,' the man in the ski mask said.

'Why not?'

'Where do you think you are?'

'London,' Megan replied. As soon as the word came out of her mouth, she knew that it was the wrong reply. She had lost all sense of time over the last few days, and she had noticed a change in the temperature. A lot of the time, it was too warm.

'Guess again,' the man said.

'You haven't had time to get me to Burma.' Megan tried to make a joke of the situation. But her captor wasn't joking.

'You were asleep for a long time,' he said.

'What day is it?'

'You were asleep for a long time,' he repeated.

'Am I really in Burma?'

'Here.' He handed a her a tray with more crappy juice, some fluffy white rice and a thin, curried sauce. 'Eat.'

When he was gone, Megan realized how hungry she was. The change in temperature, the change in the style of food. It was pretty obvious what had happened.

How could they have got her to Burma? Stupid question.

Her cell was a container. It could easily have been loaded onto a ship. If Megan had been given a strong enough sedative, she could have been out for days . . .

But why would they do that? Presumably, the video she made had been released to the world's media. If KI had withdrawn from Burma, as Megan had asked, she would be free now. So they must have decided not to withdraw.

In which case, taking Megan to Burma, imprisoning her there, just as the military imprisoned the country's last elected leader, made a kind of sense. Megan would make a good propaganda tool.

Henry/Phil wasn't here. He was back in the UK. Her jailer was Burmese. He would have no reason to feel sympathetic towards her. Until a few minutes ago, Megan believed she was going to get out soon. Now her incarceration was open-ended.

ATHENS

'Do you know this man?' Luke asked the manager, handing him a photo of his father taken the year before. They had registered in Flick's name, so the hotel had no way of knowing that Luke shared his father's surname. The picture showed a smiling Jack Kite in a short-sleeved shirt.

'Of course,' the Byron's manager replied. 'It is Mr Kite.'

'Have you seen him recently?'

'You have not heard? Mr Kite was killed in an accident.'

'I know that, yes. But when did he last stay here?'

'Mr Kite was not often in Athens, and he could afford the

very best hotels, but he did stay here with a friend, last year.'

'Mrs Jackson?'

'The French lady, yes. Why do you want to know all this? Are you perhaps related to Mr Kite? There is a resemblance.'

'I'm his son,' Luke replied. 'Is Mrs Jackson in?'

The manager checked the keys behind him. He seemed to be looking at Room 24, on the floor below Luke and Flick.

'Not at the moment, no.'

'How long is she staying for?'

'As long as she wants. At this time of year, we are not very busy. Would you like me to give her a message when she returns?'

'No, thank you. We want to surprise her.'

'I need a shower,' Flick told Luke. 'See you upstairs.'

Luke sat at the laptop in the lobby and checked his webmail. There was a note from Crystal and a couple of links from Andy. He sent his friend a cheerful reply, without revealing where he was. He ignored the message from his mother.

'You found me.' The soft voice belonged to Celine Michel, who kissed Luke on the forehead. 'I came in just now and thought, that looks like a young Jack. Why are you here?'

'You gave me that postcard, remember?'

'Of course.'

Luke logged off the computer. 'Perhaps we could talk somewhere more private.'

'Come to my room.'

Luke followed Celine to the second floor. Celine's room overlooked the street. Otherwise, it was identical to Luke and

Flick's room: spacious and functional, with raffia mats on a tiled floor and two single beds.

'Are you here alone?' Celine asked.

'No, I'm with my girlfriend.'

'Has your sister been freed yet?'

Luke shook his head.

'Oh, Luke, I'm so sorry. You must be terribly worried.'

'I am. And I'm at risk myself. That's part of the reason I came here, to get out of the UK. You may want to keep your distance from me.'

'Let me be the judge of that.'

'I thought it wasn't safe for you to travel?' Luke said.

'It's safe enough for now. After seeing those men try to snatch you, I began to think that I was at more risk in Nice.'

'You saw that?'

'Yes, but before I could do anything, it was over and you had been rescued. Who tried to kidnap you?'

'I don't know.' So much had happened in the last few days that it was hard for Luke to keep track. 'You're calling yourself Jackson. Why?'

'Paranoia. That would be an appropriate name for you, wouldn't it? Jack's son.'

'Most people, including Flick, think that I'm my father's nephew.' Luke explained why. 'Can we stick to that in public?'

'Whatever you say,' Celine said.

'Surely you can't mean to have your baby in Athens?'

'That's months away. I will return to France when it's safe.'

'Who might be after you? The people who took Megan?'

171

'Maybe. If they know I am having your father's child, then I am, they may think, connected with the Kite empire.'

'Not only them. The people running KI may be very happy to have you, and me, out of the way. That's another part of why I decided to come here.'

He explained everything that had happened in some detail. Celine was shocked.

'Who is on your side? Who is looking after you? I'm sorry, Luke, but you are still a boy. Your father is gone. He told me what your mother is like. Your uncle is in prison and the company is not on your side. You must feel so alone.'

'Not really. I've got you. And I've got Flick.'

'How did you get together with her?'

Luke told the story, then looked at his watch. 'Actually, she'll be worried about me. Shall we go and meet her?'

'I haven't told you about my search for your father yet.'

'I'm sorry. What is there to tell?'

'Not much. I have showed his photo everywhere. A few people think they've seen him. I am meeting someone later on, on an island not far from Athens. Perhaps you would accompany me.'

'Sure. What information does this person have?'

'He rang me at the hotel this morning. Said he had a message from Jack, but he needed to meet somewhere discreet.'

'That sounds too good to be true,' Luke said. 'When are we going?'

'Tonight.'

172

Thirty-Three

Megan wished she'd read the literature the BMFF gave her in London more carefully. She was in South-East Asia and needed to know something about the terrain. There was no TV here, never mind a DVD player. Her new jailer, she was starting to realize, had only basic English. She wondered whether he was part of the BMFF, or a local who was being paid to hold her.

The BMFF had tried to convert her by by having Henry/Phil position himself as a kind of pseudo-boyfriend. Could she do the same to her new jailer in return, win some favours? It had to be worth a try.

Megan cleaned herself up the best she could without a mirror. The next time he came, she remembered to smile.

'Thank you so much.'

'You're welcome.'

Megan brushed his arm lightly. 'Please. Stay and talk with me. I'm lonely.'

'Not allowed, sorry.'

'That's a pity.' She let her hand linger on his forearm.

'Maybe for a minute or two.'

'I know you're not allowed to tell me your name but, can I ask, are you Burmese?'

'No. But I have Burmese blood.'

'Ah, I see. I have a little Scottish blood, but I'm mostly English. What are you?'

'I cannot say.'

'There's no need for you to keep that mask on all the time,' she said. 'I promise not to describe you to anyone.'

'That is nice of you, but . . .'

'Please, I want to see your face. Henry let me see his face. Allow me.'

He was a polite young man and he did not flinch when Megan grabbed his ski mask, then yanked it up and over his head. Beneath it she found a man not much older, taller or heavier than her. Was he the only thing standing between her and escape?

'You're nice,' she said. 'What's your name?'

'Syu.'

'Tell me more about yourself, Syu.'

AEGINA, GREECE

The hydrofoil took under an hour. Aegina was a working island. The guidebook said that many Athenians had second homes there. In the morning, they planned to hire a car and explore before catching a hydrofoil or ferry back to Athens.

They were booked in to the Brown hotel, at the far end of the seafront. The three took a cab there, then walked back along the front. Even out of season, Aegina Town was a bustling place. There were plenty of restaurants and bars.

Celine chose a small place next to the fish market. She and Flick drank retsina, while Luke stuck to 7Up. Flick went to use the toilet.

'She's older than I expected,' Celine said. 'How old is she, twenty? Twenty-one?'

'No, she's eighteen, only a couple of years older than me.'

Celine raised an eyebrow. 'Even two years is a lot at your age. But she seems to treat you well.'

'Yes.'

'I don't think she should come to our meeting. It might not be cool. I'm not even sure I should be bringing you. But you are Jack's son, so . . .'

'Where are we meeting?'

'Beyond our hotel, five minutes past the bend in the road, there is a small residential area called Faros. Very quiet at this time of year. I am to meet my contact there at eleven.'

'And you were planning to go there alone?'

Celine shrugged. 'It may be a trap. But I carry these.' She opened her bag to reveal a can of mace, a rape alarm and a flick knife. 'Anybody who threatens me or my baby will not have an easy fight.'

Celine was a feisty woman. They seemed to be the type that Dad went for. Flick returned.

'What's in the bag?' she asked, as Celine closed it.

'Nothing important,' Celine insisted.

'At what point are you two going to explain why we've come to this island? I mean, it's nice enough. According to the guidebook, there's a temple that we can visit tomorrow. But, out of season, there's the town and the temple, not a lot else.'

'I'll explain later,' Celine said. 'Luke and I have to meet someone.'

'You and Luke, but not me?'

'It's about my father,' Luke explained. 'I don't even know if I'm going to be allowed at the meeting yet.'

He lowered his voice. 'Do you recognize that guy?'

Flick glanced at the man sitting at the next plastic table. He was thirtyish, with a heavy black beard and a matching, long leather jacket. 'No. Should I?'

'I think he was on the hydrofoil earlier.'

'Hardly surprising to find him here, then.'

'He could be following us.'

'You're being paranoid,' Flick told him.

'If you were me, you'd have every reason to be paranoid.'

They finished their meal quickly, paid the bill and returned to the hotel. While they walked along the seafront, Luke kept glancing back. He was pretty certain that they weren't followed.

'I'm shattered,' Flick said, back in their room. 'That walk up to the Parthenon this morning did me in. If you go out on your own, please be careful. Remember what happened when you last spent time alone with Celine.'

'I remember,' Luke said. 'Have you checked your phone? Is there a signal?'

She looked. 'One bar, flickering into two. You?'

Luke got out his. 'Looks OK.' He tried Flick's number, to be sure. Almost ten seconds later, it began to ring.

'If we run into any difficulties, I'll call you. But most likely nobody will turn up and I'll be back within an hour, hacked off.'

'And I'll be fast asleep,' Flick said. 'Just take good care.'

He kissed her on the forehead, then joined Celine. She, too, looked tired. It was a quarter to eleven, late for a woman who was several months pregnant.

The walk was shorter than he'd thought, which was good, because Celine moved slowly. They crossed a wide road, turned a corner and passed an internet café that was closed for the season. Soon, they saw the Faros Hotel up ahead, a wide, white building, with a single light shining from its downstairs bar.

'Looks like it's closed,' Luke said.

'I was told to wait in the bar.'

'Who by?'

'Text message.'

'How did they get your phone number?' Luke asked.

'I handed it round in a lot of places,' Celine admitted.

'Aegina's a long way to come based on one text.'

'You flew all the way to Athens because of one postcard!'

'Also because I had to get away. With Megan gone, the kidnappers might come after me.'

They walked into the bar. The single light they'd seen came from above the fridge. Chairs were stacked on top of tables. Luke checked the time on his mobile. Five to eleven. He took down a couple of chairs and they sat.

Nobody appeared. Luke felt awkward. He was in a country he didn't know with a woman he hardly knew at a bar that didn't appear to be open. He checked the time again. Still five to eleven.

'I can't see it,' Luke told Celine.

'Can't see what?'

'A set of circumstances under which Dad would fake his own death then summon us here for a meeting months later.'

'Perhaps Jack didn't fake his own death. Perhaps he was kidnapped, like your sister. Anyway, I didn't say that your father summoned us here. I said that someone . . .' She stopped because a new text was flashing on her phone. She opened it, and showed it to Luke. It was in English.

YOU WERE SUPPOSED TO COME ALONE.

'Did they specify that?' Luke asked.

She shook her head, then typed out a reply.

THIS IS JACK'S SON, LUKE. HE HAS A RIGHT TO HEAR WHAT YOU HAVE TO SAY BUT WILL LEAVE IF YOU WANT. Celine pressed *send*.

They waited. Nobody came. They waited some more. Luke looked at his watch. Eight minutes past eleven.

'How long shall we give it?' he asked Celine.

'As long as it takes,' she said.

There was a noise from behind the bar. A youth not much older than Luke appeared. He wore a white T-shirt and jeans.

'Closed,' he said.

'We're meeting someone,' Luke told him.

The youth turned on a light, flooding the room with fluorescence. Celine blinked. For the first time this evening, Luke could see how tired she was, how scared. The youth came out from behind the bar. He had steely-blue eyes, jet-black hair and pitted skin. 'Closed,' he repeated.

'They're friends of mine, Nikos,' said a new, deep, English voice, which added something in Greek. The stranger was seventyish, with thick grey hair and a full beard the same colour. He was about Luke's height, wearing a dark-green T-shirt beneath a light-coloured safari suit that had seen better days. He held out his hand.

'John Turner,' he said.

First Celine, then Luke shook his hand. At Turner's instruction, Nikos fetched a small bottle of something called ouzo, a jug of iced water and three glasses. John thanked him and poured them each a measure of the clear spirit. He added a little water to his. The drink at once turned cloudy white. Luke followed suit, then sipped at it. Aniseed-flavoured alcohol. Celine stuck to iced water.

'Why did you ask me to come here?' she asked.

'You're French?' John Turner asked. 'We can speak in French if you prefer.'

'English is fine. Luke has very little French.'

'I heard you were going round Athens asking after Jack Kite. I knew that we would need privacy and that this bar would be dead,' John smiled. 'It's not too late for you, I hope?'

Luke glanced at the swelling in Celine's belly.

Celine smiled. 'Not for me, but . . .'

'You're . . . ?'

Celine nodded.

'It's Jack's?'

Again, she nodded. The old man's eyes watered. 'Does he know?'

'I didn't have the chance to tell him before . . .'

John finished the sentence for her. 'His helicopter went down.'

'Have you heard anything since then?' Luke asked.

John didn't reply. He sipped his ouzo, lost in thought.

'Do you know anything about a postcard sent from the Byron Hotel?' Celine asked. 'It looked like Jack's handwriting. It just said "Come".'

'Yes,' John said. 'I sent that.'

'Why?' Luke asked, confused.

'Because Jack asked me to.'

'When?'

'I can't answer that. Jack made all kinds of preparations for different eventualities. I agreed to help him. I didn't know that you were pregnant or I might not have asked you to come all this way. Nevertheless, you are here, so . . .'

He sipped some more ouzo.

'There's an island near here called Angistri. Famous for its nudist beach and for having very little law enforcement. A wanted terrorist hid there for months before being found.'

'Are you saying that that is where——?' Celine began.

'I'm saying that it might be a good place to not be found. Jack had . . . has enemies. If you were to wait on Angistri, he would know where to find you. And I would be nearby, should there be any problem. I speak good Greek and have many local contacts. Perhaps you would like to think about it.'

He handed Celine a map, on which were written an address and phone number. He pointed. 'I live on the next street. A second-floor flat. Come and see me at midday tomorrow if you would like me to take you to Angistri.'

'Both of us?'

'That's up to you. I would walk you back to your hotel. However, it's probably best that we aren't seen together.'

Luke remembered his paranoia about the bearded bloke in the café earlier. But it was only paranoia. Why would anybody follow them here?

'I still have many questions I have to ask you!' Celine said.

'Which I cannot answer yet. You'll have to trust me, I'm afraid. I'm keeping a promise to an old friend.'

'Very well. Until tomorrow, then.'

All the way back to the hotel, Luke and Celine discussed John Turner and what his connection with Jack Kite might be.

'A relative, perhaps?'

'They're all dead, apart from Mike in prison and a grandma with Alzheimer's in a nursing home. Thing is, I didn't see Dad a lot. I don't know much about his friends.'

'Do you want to hide out on this island?'

'I'm not sure how long my money would last, or what Flick would think about it.'

'Let's sleep on it,' Celine suggested.

They agreed to meet for breakfast at nine.

Thirty-Four

Megan didn't know when or where Syu slept or if he worked shifts, but he was the only guy she ever saw. Each mealtime, he spent a little more time talking to her.

'Have they released the video yet?' she asked.

'I don't know anything about a video.'

'Do you have the internet here?'

'Yes, we have the internet. There are many restrictions, of course.' Megan tried not to show a reaction to this. It was the nearest he'd come to confirming that they were in Burma, where the government kept the internet under tight control.

'Could I look at some websites? I'm so starved of news. I've run out of things to read. I'm really lonely. Having the internet would help.'

'I'm sorry.'

'Perhaps you could at least let me send an email or two. I have friends who will be very worried about me: my cousin, my boyfriend and his sister. Please. It would mean a great deal to me.' She gave him her warmest smile. 'I'd be very cooperative.'

'I will ask. I doubt they will say yes. We have only one laptop computer with internet access.'

'A mobile phone would do.'

Syu hesitated. 'I will do my best to help you.'

'Thank you so much.' Megan leaned over and pressed her body against his as she kissed him on the cheek. Syu blushed, then left quickly, not forgetting to bolt the door behind him.

AEGINA, GREECE

When Luke got up, Flick wasn't in the hotel. She must have got up early and gone for a walk so as not to wake him. Odd, because most days she needed more sleep than he did. No time to worry. He was already late for breakfast with Celine. Luke dressed quickly and hurried down to the dining room. Celine was at a table on her own, eating fruit and yoghurt.

'Have you seen Flick?' he asked.

'No.'

'She wasn't there when I woke up.'

'Should we be worried?'

'I don't think so.' Luke ordered breakfast. They looked at a map of Angistri and talked about John Turner's proposal.

'I don't think I can stay on Angistri,' Celine said. 'If anything went wrong, I'd be way too far from a hospital.'

'Maybe we should visit Angistri before we leave, though. I got the feeling that John Turner knows a lot more than he was saying. It's possible that, if we got to the island . . .' Luke didn't want to say, 'We'll find my dad there' – he still thought that Celine was clinging to a false hope. Instead, he finished the sentence, 'We'll find out more about what's been going on.'

'Yes, I suppose.'

'You look depressed,' Luke said. 'What's wrong?'

'Secretly, I hoped to see Jack here. Last night, when I worked out that it was Jack's writing on the card, but John posted it . . .' Her words trailed off.

'Listen,' Luke said, trying to reassure her. 'Since coming here, meeting John Turner, I've changed my mind. For the first time, I'm beginning to think that Dad really is alive.'

'I've always been sure that he's alive,' Celine said. 'But today, I'm feeling tired. Maybe it's time for me to go home.'

'OK,' Luke said. 'I'll see if I can persuade Flick to visit Angistri with me before we go back to Athens. I'm in the opposite situation to you. It's not safe for me to go home.'

'Surely you have protection from KI, Special Branch, Interpol even . . . One of their agents helped you in Nice, *oui*?'

'Yes. It's KI that I don't trust. I think they'd be happy if I was out of the way because . . .'

His mobile began to ring. Flick.

'Hi. Where are you?'

'I . . . I had an early breakfast and went for a walk. Is Celine with you?'

'Yes.'

'There's something I want to show you both. Did you pass an internet café last night?'

'Yes.'

'That's where I am. Come and meet me, both of you.'

'I thought it had closed for the season.'

'No, I'm in here. I've . . . I've found something out.'

'OK, give us ten minutes or so.'

Luke shoved his phone back into the inside pocket of his

cotton jacket, where it fell through a hole in the lining. He was in too much of a hurry to fish it out. As soon as he had relayed the conversation to Celine, they set off along the coast road.

The day was starting to heat up. Luke looked across the Saronic Sea. That island in the distance, was it Angistri? There were no buildings in sight. He thought about the map they'd looked at over breakfast. It wasn't a tiny island, but had only a handful of roads, a few little settlements, and large swathes of uncultivated land. A man could easily get lost there.

'This place still looks closed to me,' Celine said.

The internet café was a ugly, modern building, on the edge of a car park. A white van was parked at its rear. The café's grey concrete walls were unpainted. The door was metal, with no window.

'This doesn't feel right to me. Luke, wait!'

Luke ignored Celine. His girlfriend was waiting for them. He pushed the door open. Inside, it was dark.

'Flick?'

In half-light, he could make out computers, but no people.

'I don't like this,' Celine said. 'I think we should get out.'

Too late. The metal door slammed behind them. Luke tried the handle, but the door would no longer open.

A light came on.

'Flick?'

The light was not from the area with the computers, but from a doorway beyond. Two men stood there. Both wore masks. The one who spoke had good English.

'Do not be afraid. We are not going to harm you. We are with the BMFF.'

Luke tried to push his way past them into the light. There had to be an exit at the back. The men grabbed him roughly.

'Do not resist or we will hurt the women.'

Luke let his arms go slack. They tied Luke and Celine's hands behind their backs, blindfolded them, then put them into the back of the white van they had seen earlier.

'Where's Flick?' Luke kept asking.

He got no reply. Before the van set off, one of the men searched him.

'Phone?'

'I left it at the hotel,' Luke lied. The guy missed the slim bulge in the bottom corner of his jacket. He gagged Luke and Celine, then covered them with heavy canvas, giving them no room to move.

The van made a short journey. When it stopped, Luke could tell what was happening. He recognized the noises. They had driven along the seafront to the port of Aegina. The van was getting onto a ferry. From Aegina Town, ferries went to many places, including Athens, where they had come from, and Angistri.

A deep rumble began beneath them. They were in motion.

Thirty-Five

GREECE

The van went fast, bouncing Luke and Celine around. Hard to keep track of time or sense how far they had gone. Was this what it had been like for Megan? Luke was doing his best not to think about her. It was wisest not to get too attached to people, he decided. Not Celine and her unborn child. Not even Flick. He didn't want to know what they had done to her.

Luke's mobile phone was turned on. He had it set to a loud ring for calls and vibrate for texts. If it rang, his captors were bound to hear and confiscate it.

Luke's hands were tied. There was nothing he could do to turn off the ringer. He felt it vibrate once, which meant a text arriving. Not many people had his latest number: Andy, Ethan, Grace, Megan, Flick, Ian and, since last night, Celine. Nobody at KI, because he didn't trust any of them. Certainly not his mom. She had the Barbican phone number and that of an old mobile he'd lost track of. Presumably, Flick had been taken too, although she wasn't with them. So she wouldn't be calling. The person most likely to ring was Ethan, in London, to update him on the situation there. With luck, he would do this in a text.

Luke's new phone had a long battery life when it was on standby. Maybe, at some point, he'd get the chance to use it.

He tried to hold on to that thought. The van stopped. It had stopped several times before, but this time it didn't start again. Five minutes later, he heard the van doors opening. Gentle hands picked him up and pulled him out. He was untied, but still gagged and blindfolded. Not that he was in any state to run. His limbs were stiff and one foot had gone to sleep. He could barely stand.

The gag came off. 'Where am I?' Luke said. 'Where's Flick?'

'It doesn't matter where you are. Your girlfriend is safe. We did not need to bring her. She will be freed if you cooperate. I will take off your blindfold now, as long as you promise to behave sensibly.'

'I promise,' Luke said.

His captor was the bearded guy from the restaurant. A thin guy in long shorts was untying Celine.

'All of the doors are locked,' their bearded captor said. 'If you try to escape, we will have to hurt you and tie you up again. Do not make us do that. We are peaceful people.'

Luke nodded acceptance. He heard Celine moan. Her gag must have been taken off. She spoke, first in French, then, when that got no response, in English.

'I need a bathroom. I am pregnant. A bathroom, please.'

Both men had to help her. Luke got a moment to himself. He believed them when they said that all of the doors were locked, but he had time to dig his phone out of his jacket lining, put it on *silent* and read his new text before shoving the phone down his jeans. It was more accessible there and only a very intimate search would find it. The text read: I THINK I'M IN BURMA. A GUARD CALLED SYU WILL HELP ME ESCAPE BUT NEEDS MONEY TO PAY BRIBES. YOU CAN FIND HIM AT

Luke didn't have time to memorize the address she'd written, but his phone recognized the sender. Either somebody was messing with his mind, or his sister was still alive.

ISLINGTON, LONDON

'You are *not* flying to Burma!' Ethan's mum told him. 'After what happened to Megan, you mustn't even consider it.'

'She's there. She needs my help.'

'You got a text message. It proves nothing.'

Grace was right. It could be that somebody was playing a sick game. The message wasn't sent from Megan's phone and finished DONT REPLY TO THIS – she had used all one hundred and sixty characters that the text message allowed, and she only *thought* she was in Burma. Ethan had looked up the brief address she had given. It was a street address in Rangoon, the capital of Burma. Or Yangon, as the military dictatorship called the city.

'I have to go,' Ethan said.

'I'm coming with you,' Grace insisted.

'No!' Mum insisted. 'I absolutely forbid it. You both have university. It's pointless and dangerous. There are elections coming up. The army will be on the streets. There'll be

189

violence. I don't want you there, either of you.'

'It's not your decision,' Ethan said. 'It's mine. I've got to help Megan.'

'There are people better qualified to do that. KI's security force . . .'

'Look what happened when they tried before! I thought Megan probably *was* killed!'

'I didn't want to say this,' Mum said, 'but Megan was probably killed in that accidental explosion. Someone is luring you into a trap. What about her cousin? You tell me she shared half her fortune with him. He must have the resources to—'

'He's gone on holiday with Flick. I texted him just now but there's been no reply yet.'

'Mum, we need to go,' Grace said. 'Anyway, we'd be on the junta's side. They're hardly going to arrest us, are they?'

'I absolutely forbid it, and if either of you try to go, I swear I'll cancel your credit cards!'

Grace was already up to the limit on her card, Ethan knew, but his had a higher limit due to his gap year travels. Still, his family paid the bills and his parents could easily cancel the card. He had to appear to play along.

'Ring Ian Trevelyan,' Mum said. 'Tell him what the text said and get the British Embassy in Burma to look into it.'

'I'll do that,' Ethan said.

Grace went off in a sulk. Ethan guessed she was angry that Megan had texted him and not her. She resented him stealing her best friend. If he took Grace to Burma with him, it might heal the rift in their relationship, but Mum was right, it could be dangerous. Grace still had trouble walking long distances. If anything else happened to her, his parents would never forgive him. Whereas if anything happened to him, they'd still have Grace.

Once he was alone, Ethan checked flights online. There were two changes and the flight took about a day, but he had enough credit, so he booked the next available trip.

Only when he was at the airport did he ring Ian Trevelyan at Special Branch.

'Are there any developments?' he asked.

'They haven't found any bodies, if that's what you want to know. The only indications that she's dead are that the BMFF haven't sent out the video and what your friend Panya said.'

'I saw Panya last night and asked her about that again. She said she heard somebody died, but she may have jumped to conclusions.'

Ethan didn't know what had really gone on in Panya's mind. She had exaggerated what she'd been told, that much was clear. And she'd been there to comfort him.

Last night, drowning his sorrows, he'd had a lot to drink and spent the night at hers. This morning, he'd got Megan's text and felt awful. He'd shown Panya the text. That was when she told him that she couldn't be sure that Megan was dead.

'If Panya's changed her story, that's a good sign,' Ian said.

'Are KI withdrawing from Burma?'

'I'm not privy to KI's plans, but I would guess not. They seem to be assuming that Megan's dead and trying to keep the whole thing hush hush. It'll blow up in their faces at some point, but they appear to be prepared to put up with the bad publicity. Do you have any information for me?'

'As a matter of fact, I do.' Ethan told Ian about the text.

'The style of the message,' Ian said, 'does it sound like Megan?'

'Yes, it does.'

'I'll get on to our embassy in Burma. Have them look into it. I don't want you to raise your hopes. These kidnappers aren't well organized. I find it hard to believe that they'd manage to smuggle Megan to Burma. But if she is there, it could represent an incredible publicity coup for them. Is there anything else?'

'Not at the moment,' Ethan said. If he told Ian that he was about to set off to Burma, Special Branch might find a way to intercept him. Best to let him know when he arrived.

Ethan turned off his mobile. Grace thought he was at Panya's. She didn't approve of him spending so much time with her so soon after Megan's death, but she'd give an alibi to their parents if asked. When his sister found out what he was really doing, he hoped it would make up for what had gone wrong between them.

GREECE

The kidnappers were surprisingly relaxed, almost friendly. They also spoke some English.

'Is Flick still on Aegina?' Luke asked.

'She is safe. That is all I can tell you.'

'And what do I have to do for you to release her?'

'Nothing.'

'Nothing?'

'We have every blood member of your family except for the one who is in a US prison.'

Did they know that the child Celine was pregnant with was Dad's? Surely there was no way they could have found that out.

'Your company will have to meet our demands if they want us to release you. Today, all I ask you to do is hold up this newspaper.'

He handed Luke a copy of the *International Herald Tribune*.

'Open it on page ten.'

Luke did. The headline read *Burmese Junta to announce election date*. Luke showed the story to Celine.

'What is happening in Burma has nothing to do with me,' she told their captors. 'I sympathize with your aims, but the people at KI don't even know I exist. Kidnapping me is a waste of your time.'

'That is for us to decide.'

'People will not be sympathetic to your cause when they find out that you kidnapped a pregnant woman.'

'We are not interested in sympathy,' the kidnapper said, turning on a digital camera. 'We are interested in results.'

'Let's get it over with,' Luke said.

He and Celine held the paper open between them.

The camera flashed twice.

Luke spoke. 'We've posed for you, now do something for me. You said that you have every blood member of my family so I repeat, you must know – is my sister still alive?'

'Your girlfriend will be released shortly. As for your sister, it would have been in the media if she was dead, yes?'

The kidnappers left them. Luke tried to think. He'd never believed that Megan was dead, but now it had been confirmed: she was alive and wanted him to come and help her. Flick was about to be freed. When KI found out that the kidnappers had all of the Kite family, what would their reaction be? Would they send in another armed squad, risking death and destruction to rescue them? No, that was the wrong question. The question should be: who benefited? If he, Megan and Celine were to die, who would inherit the company? Luke had made no will. Everything of Megan's came to him. If all three of them were gone, there was only one family member left to inherit.

Uncle Mike.

Thirty-Six

Megan knew she could have said more, but hadn't had any time to think it through beforehand. She wasn't expecting Syu to have her own phone. He only let her use it for a few minutes. Syu had opened a window for a new text message before handing it to her, so she didn't get to check her messages. She'd selected Ethan and Luke from her list of contacts, then got as much information as she could into the one-hundred-and-sixty-character limit.

Immediately afterwards, Syu deleted the sent message. 'I must return this before it is missed,' he had said, and hurried out.

When he next came, she tried to ask him how much money he would need to help her escape.

'A thousand US dollars,' he said.

It didn't sound like much. You could withdraw that kind of sum in a couple of trips to a cash machine.

'And for that, you would get me to the British Embassy?'

'If that is where you want to go. We may need more money to pay off guards.'

'How much more?'

'One, two hundred dollars.'

'My cousin or my boyfriend would be able to pay that.

They're the people I texted.'

'Good.'

'How will one of them find you if you're not at the address I gave them?'

'Someone there will send a message. They will find me.'

'I don't want you to get into trouble.'

'You pay me. I take a little risk. Probably no trouble. If I get arrested, you will speak for me, yes?'

'Of course.'

Syu nodded.

'Very well then.'

When he opened and closed the door on his way out, she thought she could hear a storm. It must be the rainy season.

GREECE

Luke and Celine sat on the garage floor, leaning against the white van. Their legs were tied but their arms were free. The bearded kidnapper had been watching them from a chair opposite, but had just gone into a back room.

Luke's left foot had gone to sleep. He squirmed, trying to get some life back into it. In doing so, he woke up Celine, who had been dozing for half an hour.

'What do you think's going on?' he asked her. 'Do you reckon they know what they're doing?'

'I don't think they will hurt your girlfriend,' Celine said. 'But I can't stand this for long.'

'Did they take your phone?'

'Yes. I thought you didn't have yours?'

'It was caught in the lining of my jacket. They missed it.' He told her about the text from Megan.

'That's great, if it's real,' Celine said. 'But you must phone for help. Quickly! One of them is bound to return soon.'

Luke got out the phone. He still had a signal. There were three missed calls. It was a good thing he'd left it on *silent*.

He had no idea what number to call. Dialling nine-nine-nine might take him through to local emergency services, but he didn't speak Greek or have the time to hang around waiting for a translator to be found. So he called Ian Trevelyan. The call took precious seconds to go through. When it connected, however, it was answered on the first ring.

'Luke. Where are you?'

'Greece, according to the service provider status on my phone. Other than that, I don't know. Celine and I have been kidnapped by a Greek branch of the BMFF. I don't know how long we've got before they return.'

'Since when have they been holding you?'

'They took us just after ten this morning. We were on an island not far from Athens. I think they took us on a ferry to the mainland and we drove for some time after that.'

'If you keep your mobile switched on, Interpol should be able to trace the signal and find you. Can you do that?'

'Yes, there's enough battery to last a couple of days if I don't make calls. Ian, I hear someone coming. 'I've got to go.'

'Call me again if you get the chance.'

Luke stuffed the phone back down his jeans. The bearded guy brought in bread, jam and yoghurt. When they'd eaten, Celine asked if she could have a wash.

'No.'

'Where are we supposed to sleep?' Celine asked.

'I will bring you blankets,' their captor said.

'We would like to know when you are going to free us. We would like to know when you will free our friend, Flick.'

'I may have answers for you in the morning.'

When the guy had gone, Luke looked around the garage. Its roof was merely corrugated iron, yet it looked secure. Even if Luke could find something to stand on, he wouldn't have any chance of forcing an opening. The garage doors were firmly locked from the outside. The only thing he could use as a weapon was the wooden chair their kidnappers sat in to watch them from. The chair might hurt someone if Luke hit them with it, but it wasn't strong enough to smash a way out.

The bearded guy returned and unlocked the rear of the van. Then he untied their legs. Celine and Luke got back into the van, resuming the positions they'd been in for the journey from Aegina.

'I have to lock you inside,' the guy said. 'There's bottled water and you should have enough air. Also, there are blankets you can use if you get cold.'

'I need a bathroom,' Celine complained.

'In the morning.'

He locked the van door behind them. They were left in the dark.

It was starting to get cold. At least they weren't tied up. They huddled together for warmth.

There was no way to get from the back of the van into the front. Luke entertained a fantasy of breaking out of the back, finding the van keys in the ignition and driving through the garage doors to safety. But the fantasy fell down at every level.

They were stuck.

Their prison grew darker and colder. Luke and Celine wrapped themselves in blankets, then talked in the dark to keep their spirits up. She told him about growing up in France, moving to Nice, meeting his father. Luke told her about how he came to be born, Uncle Mike, and the mess that he and Megan had gotten into earlier in the year.

'Trouble seems to attract you, Luke Kite.'

'Not just me. My whole family. Do you think I should call Ian again?'

'Shhhh!' Celine hissed, then lowered her voice. 'One of the kidnappers may still be outside, guarding us. It's too risky. The important thing is that the phone is switched on, sending out a signal that Interpol can trace. Yes?'

Luke pulled the phone out of his jeans. Earlier it had shown two bars, which meant it had half a charge left.

It was down to one. Luke remembered that, when the phone was about to run out of power, it sounded a piercing whine every five minutes until it died. He didn't know whether it made that noise when it was on *silent*. There was nothing he could do about it, so he decided not to tell Celine. She was worried enough already.

RANGOON, BURMA

Mingaladon International Airport was the quietest, emptiest international airport Ethan had visited, but it worked efficiently. The only delay came when he had to have his bag X-rayed. He checked his phone once he was in the Arrivals concourse. No signal.

The currency was the kyat, six to the euro. Ethan had checked online before leaving. There were no cash machines and credit cards weren't much use here. The only foreign currency most places accepted was US dollars. He had changed five hundred pounds into dollars before leaving. He hoped it would be enough. He didn't intend to stay long.

The taxi driver spoke some English. Ethan negotiated a ten-dollar fee for the sixteen kilometres into the city centre. He'd travelled in Asia before and was used to bad roads and rundown buildings. Burma was as bad as any place he'd seen.

'Good time to visit,' his driver said. 'Rainy season ending.'

'Great,' Ethan said.

They passed at least a dozen soldiers and one army convoy. However, when they got to the city, Rangoon (or Yangon, as the junta would have it), it was surprisingly free of military. He checked in to the Central Hotel on Bogyoke Aung San Street, where they gave him a single room for thirty dollars a night.

'How long you staying?'

'Two nights, maybe three.'

Ethan explored the city at night. There were plenty of

buildings left by the British. He spotted the old High Court and, in the middle of a roundabout, the famous Sule Pagoda. A lot of the colonial buildings were dilapidated and fenced off. The British Embassy was closed. It was near the Yangon river and the colonial style Strand Hotel, which was well lit and seemed to have been fully restored. If he and Megan were on holiday here, this is where they would stay, Ethan figured, a classic Englishman Abroad haunt. But this wasn't a holiday.

Burma was six and a half hours ahead of the UK. Ethan, who had slept a little on the plane, felt discombobulated. He ate some noodles and spicy beef at ten, then went to his room, but couldn't sleep. There was a curfew at eleven. It was too risky to go out again. He pored over a map he'd bought, trying to locate the address Megan had sent him. It was no use. He would have to ask at the embassy. And tomorrow, he might meet the guy he had to bribe: Syu.

Thirty-Seven

After Megan sent the text message, Syu came less often. Maybe he was waiting at home for somebody to come with the bribe. The other guard who appeared looked more Pakistani than Burmese. That's to say he didn't look much like the Burmese people in the films she'd been made to watch. But what did Megan know? The guard had no inclination to talk to her, and wouldn't even reveal his name when she talked to him.

'How long am I going to be here? Has that video I made been sent out? What happened to Henry?'

Never a word in reply. Food no longer arrived frequently. There were no newspapers or magazines for her to read. Megan thought about the hostages she'd heard about, but the stories blurred in her mind. John McCarthy, Terry Waite, Brian Keenan – what country were they held in? Somewhere in the Middle East. At least, she thought, they had had each other for company. She could take the hunger, the smell, the feeling grubby all the time. It was the loneliness that was killing her.

To take her mind off the situation, Megan exercised relentlessly. She did press-ups, stretches, squats, running on the spot. It was hard, especially when there wasn't enough to eat or drink and she only had a flannel and bottled water to wash with. The exercise and some yoga helped her to chill out – a little. She could feel herself get stronger. There only seemed to be one guard on at a time. She doubted that her kidnappers would be caught out a second time. But she had to hope.

RANGOON, BURMA

Dawn was white and cold. Ethan had slept badly. He'd not closed the blinds properly, so the light woke him. He showered, hid most of his folding money in the plastic money belt he wore in dodgy areas, then put on jeans and a plain T-shirt. He wanted to dress inconspicuously, but given that he was European and most of the men here wore a kind of skirt (*longyi*, they were called) he was sure to stand out.

After breakfast, he headed to the embassy. The centre of Rangoon was laid out on a grid system, similar to New York's, so it was straightforward enough to find his way around, even in his jet-lagged state.

The embassy was still closed. It didn't open until 8 a.m. Ethan could bang on the door, claim that it was an emergency, but he didn't want to draw attention to himself. He wasn't sure, anyway, that the embassy would want to help him. He'd looked at their website before setting off. It gave the impression that the embassy staff were sympathetic to Burmese democrats. How would they feel about rescuing a British woman who had been kidnapped and smuggled into the country by pro-democracy terrorists? It would put them in an awkward situation.

Ethan knew what the British government did when faced with an awkward, embarrassing situation. As little as possible.

'Sir, you look like you need a guide!'

The guidebook had warned that tourists would be hassled by would-be guides. This guy was at least fifty. A few thin strands of hair formed a fringe over his shiny head. His blue *longyi* was badly faded.

'Maybe later,' Ethan said.

'Dear sir, you should strike while the iron is hot!'

'Sure, but . . .' Ethan reached into his pocket and pulled out the address that Megan had texted him. He showed the guide his scrap of paper. 'Do you know where this is?'

The guide frowned, curled his lip, then said, 'This is not a good area for tourists.'

'According to my guidebook, Rangoon is the safest city for tourists in all of Asia.'

'Normally maybe, but not at the moment. Also, it is quite a long way.'

'I'll get a taxi then.'

'A taxi will not take you.'

Was the guy winding him up, trying to extract money from him? Ethan didn't know. He didn't care, as long as he found the guy who had agreed to help Megan.

'How much for you to take me there?'

The guide frowned again. 'Kyat or US dollar?'

'US dollar.' Ethan still hadn't changed any money.

'Ten dollars, there and back again.'

'OK. Let's go.'

'My name is Khin. It means *friendly* in the Queen's English.'

Khin put something into his mouth. The guide had black teeth and red lips from chewing betel leaves. Seeing Ethan's interest, Khin offered him a lump of the stuff.

'Betel quid. Try some. Very good.'

'I don't think so,' Ethan said.

'Like coffee, only better for you. Protects against bacteria. Good for digestion. It is scientifically proven.'

'I don't want black teeth!' Ethan said, hoping he hadn't insulted the guide.

'In Burma, we used to say that only dogs, ghosts and Europeans have white teeth! One try will not hurt you. No?'

'No thanks.'

They left the city's grid system and the guide began to tell Ethan about the Schwedagon Pagoda, which they were going to pass on the way.

'Most famous place in Myanmar! Many tourists like to visit at dawn, for the light. We ought to go inside!'

They could see the temple complex from a distance. Khin told Ethan how the temple's central golden stupa reached a hundred metres into the sky. There were a cluster of smaller, darker stupas beneath this giant one, and an outer ring of neon-lit shrines. At some time in the fifteenth century, Khin said, a queen by the name of Shinsawbu gilded the central stupa with her own weight in gold leaf, to show her generosity and devotion. Her son-in-law later offered four times both his own weight and his wife's weight. Their descendants added more and more gold in the generations that followed. This had once been a very, very rich country. Maybe it still could be, Ethan thought, if the military weren't able to suck up all the wealth.

The place was thronged with people, few of whom looked like tourists.

'You really must take a closer look!' Khin said. 'Nobody can visit Burma without seeing the Schwedagon Pagoda.'

'I've seen it,' Ethan said. 'Let's keep moving.'

Reluctantly, the guide took him across the road, through a park, away from the gaudy, golden pagoda.

'This is People's Park,' Khin explained. 'Higher up, it becomes Resistance Park.'

'Resistance against who – the British colonialists?'

'No. The Japanese. Our resistance against them was led by General Aung San.'

The park was vast. While they crossed it, Khin gave Ethan a brief history lesson, telling him about Aung San, the assassinated Democrat whose daughter later led the Democracy Movement. She was elected Prime Minister in 1990, her party winning eighty-two percent of the vote. The army refused to hand over power. Instead, they put her under house arrest.

'How many votes do you think they will get in the new elections?' Ethan asked.

'Her party will not be allowed to stand,' Khin replied.

They reached a crossroads at the end of the park, crossed it and found themselves in an area that was kind of familiar.

'What is this, Chinatown?'

'Precisely. That is what we call these few streets. There is where you want to go. That building behind the food stall.'

'Will you not take me to the door? I might need a translator.'

'Not safe for me. I said I would bring you here and take you back, but I do not want to go to prison. I am a poor man. To live well in prison you must be rich, we always say.'

'I could really use your help over there,' Ethan said. In the last few minutes, he had come to like Khin, almost to trust him.

'Sorry, sorry. I will wait for you here under this tree.'

The building Ethan approached had a big stall in front of the entrance and no number. Without Khin's help, Ethan would never have found it. He knocked on the door and it fell open.

The wooden house was dilapidated and appeared empty. Ethan figured he must have been given the wrong address, or that the text he'd received was a hoax. Then he noticed a screen. From behind it, he heard a shuffling noise. A soft voice.

'Come, come.'

The screen was pulled back. There were two men standing there. Both wore the traditional *lyongi*. One was old, or at least middle-aged, the other maybe in his twenties.

'You have come from Kite Industries?' said the younger man.

'Not quite,' Ethan replied. 'I've come from the UK. My name's . . .'

But he didn't get to finish the sentence. Something blunt and heavy landed on his head, knocking him out.

Thirty-Eight

RANGOON, BURMA

'Where is she?' Ethan asked when he woke, the back of his head throbbing. 'Where are you holding Megan?'

'Your sister is safe,' he was told.

'She's not . . .' They thought he was Luke. Ethan tried to work out if there was any way he could play the mistaken identity to his advantage. He couldn't think of one.

'Megan Kite isn't my sister. She's my girlfriend. Where is she?'

'All in good time,' he was told. 'What is your name? Do you have your passport with you?'

It was best to carry formal identification to show the military, Ethan had been warned, so he had the passport on him. He handed it over.

'Who are you?' Ethan asked. He daren't mention the name of his contact in case he got Syu into trouble.

'Do you work for Kite Industries?' his captor asked, ignoring the question.

'No. I'm a student. Megan's my girlfriend. I have nothing to do with Kite Industries.'

'I'm afraid we will have to keep you here nevertheless.

You would not have come to this address had you not received a text message from Megan Kite.'

'That's right.' Ethan decided not to tell him that his mum was in the British government.

'I apologize for the inconvenience,' his young captor said in his very clear, slightly overprecise English, 'but I am going to have to tie you up, Ethan Thompson.'

'Then will you take me to see Megan, at least?'

'I'm afraid that may prove rather difficult.'

GREECE

Celine rested her head on Luke's chest. After a while, she dozed off. It was hard for Luke to move without disturbing her. He thought about his sister, and whether she really was alive. The BMFF could easily have hung on to her mobile and set a trap for him. If he got out of this, he ought to go back to New York, sort everything out from there.

He thought about Celine, and his little half-brother. If Luke was entitled to an equal share of the company, so was the unborn child. Both of them might be better off without. Dad used to say it wasn't money that made you happy, it was the work you did to make the money, the sense of achievement. Of course it was easy to say that when you were already rich.

He could hear sounds outside the van. A snoring guard? Luke tried to convince himself that the low battery noise would not start for at least a day. Celine groaned in her sleep. She must be having a bad dream. If Luke were asleep, he'd be having bad dreams too. Probably about what was happening to Flick.

He tried to work out what the kidnappers had done to Flick. There was no point in keeping her with him and Celine. She was of no value to KI. Her only value to the kidnappers was as a lever to get Luke to do whatever they wanted. If they found out about his phone, would they hurt Flick in retaliation? He couldn't stand it if that happened.

Luke wasn't in love with Flick. He'd seen what love did to people. It opened them up to getting hurt. Whatever was happening between them, there was too much pressure for it to be a normal relationship. Yet Flick made him happy. Happier, anyway, after all that he had been through this year.

Nearly 8 a.m. It would be light outside. Still one bar of power left. He could hear an engine, not far off. Then some rattles and banging. The noise that followed could only be the garage doors lifting open. Celine lifted her head from his chest.

'*Qu'est-ce qui se passe?*'

'I think . . .'

Shouting in Greek. Banging on the van rear door. Then one voice started to speak English.

'Luke Kite! Celine Michel! Are you in there?'

Luke and Celine began to shout back. They heard the garage door being smashed open.

Five minutes later, they were free.

'Did you catch any of the kidnappers?' Luke asked the leader of the Interpol crew.

'No. There was nobody else here. Maybe they plan

to come back later. We will have the Greek police put a guard on this site, arrest any kidnappers who return. But that's unlikely.'

'Do you think they left us there to die, or because they expected us to be rescued?'

'If I could get inside the head of terrorists, I would be a more senior detective than I am now.'

'Is there any word on my girlfriend, Flick?' Luke asked.

'According to the Brown Hotel on Aegina, she checked out yesterday. Her bags are gone and so are yours. Can you think of anywhere that she might be?'

'The Byron Hotel, by the Acropolis in Athens. We were supposed to return there.'

'Then we will take you there shortly. But I think it would be wise for you to return to the UK as soon as possible.'

It was already past midday. He and Celine were taken to a police station. They looked at photographs of terrorist suspects. None of the pictures resembled the two men they had seen without masks on. Luke kept thinking about Flick. If she had been released, why hadn't she phoned him? He checked his phone. The battery was dead.

He and Celine got to the Byron Hotel early in the evening.

'Have you seen my girlfriend?' he asked at Reception.

They hadn't.

'You mean the blonde with the high heels, yeah?' asked the teenager who had been using the hotel computer two days before, and was still camped in front of it.

'That's her.'

'I saw her leaving this morning, wheeling her bag down

211

the hill to the taxi rank.'

'How bizarre,' Celine said.

Luke thanked the guy and collected his key. Their room was empty but for his bag, which lay on the bed, packed. When he lifted the bag, there was a note beneath it.

'What does it say?' Celine asked.

Luke showed it to her:

Luke, the people who took you kept me overnight in Aegina, then sent me back here with all your stuff and Celine's. They said if I cooperated and didn't call anyone, you'd be freed. They also said they were just making a point to KI. They wanted you to know that they could get you anywhere, anytime, so KI should get out of Burma, or you've had it. I hope you're OK. I don't feel safe here, so I'm going home. Please call me when you get this.

Flick xxx

'I don't blame her for going home,' Celine said, as Luke plugged in his phone charger. 'I'm about to do the same thing.'

Flick's phone went straight to voicemail. Luke left a quick message: 'Interpol rescued us. We're back at the Byron. Call me when you get this. I don't know what I'm doing next yet, but I'll let you know when I do.'

Next, he called Ian Trevelyan. He told him about the text message he'd received, purporting to come from his sister.

'Ethan Thompson received one as well,' Ian told him. 'I've asked the British Embassy in Burma to look into it.'

'Do you think the text was genuine? Do you think Megan

really is being held hostage in Burma?'

'I don't have a firm opinion one way or the other. I do think there's a strong chance Megan is alive. If she is in Burma, I can't work out how they got her there in such a short time.'

'The BMFF still haven't shown the video?'

'No. I suspect they're saving it for a time when it will have maximum impact. Perhaps when the junta announce the Burmese elections, which could be any day now.'

Luke was hurt that Flick hadn't waited for him. If she was a proper girlfriend, she would have done. Maybe this meant she . . . no. He didn't have time to think about that yet.

Megan was his sister. Blood mattered. She needed him. He had a responsibility.

'I think I have to go over there,' Luke told Ian.

'I wouldn't advise it. Burma can be a dangerous country.'

'Don't worry,' Luke said. 'I can look after myself.'

Luke checked the planes on the hotel computer. He could leave today if he got a move on. He booked an e-ticket using his untraceable account, paid his hotel bill, then took a taxi to the airport. Once he'd checked in, he tried to ring Flick again. No reply. She couldn't still be in the air, could she? Maybe she was being questioned by Special Branch. He knew she was all right, but he wanted to know exactly what had happened to her. He needed details. He rang Ethan Thompson's number. The call went straight to voicemail. He rang Grace Thompson, the only other person he could think of that Megan might have texted,

'Grace, this is Luke.'

'I thought you were on holiday,' Grace said. 'Are you and Flick having a good time?'

'No. We aren't on holiday, we've been on a wild goose chase that ended with us both being kidnapped. Interpol freed me a few hours ago. While I was captured, I got a text message that seemed to come from Megan. Did you get one, too?'

Grace's tone changed. 'I didn't, but Ethan did. About meeting someone called Syu in Rangoon.'

'Has he done anything about it?'

'He got there last night. What are you doing?'

'I'm waiting to take a flight over there. When I arrive, I'll try to hook up with Ethan. I might be too late to help, but I have to try. I'll call you as soon as I get there and see if you have contact details for Ethan.'

'Luke, I'm worried about Ethan. He should have called by now. Mum and Dad are starting to ask questions. He promised Mum that he wouldn't go. I keep stonewalling them.'

'I'd tell your parents the truth,' Luke suggested. 'They can't blame Ethan for doing the right thing. I've got to go. They're calling my flight. I should be there in about fifteen hours. I'll call then.'

Luke walked to the boarding area and got in line.

Thirty-Nine

Syu hadn't appeared for what seemed like days. Megan's last
visitor had been over twenty-four hours ago. He'd left extra
drinking water but it was nearly all gone. The toilet needed
emptying. She had very little left to eat.

Megan didn't have the energy for vigorous exercise.
She concentrated on yoga instead. She knew a few
positions that would help keep her mind and body limber.
She wished she could remember more. How long had she
been a prisoner? It felt like a month but was probably more
like a fortnight.

If the BMFF were going to kill her, wouldn't they have
done it by now? And if KI were going to withdraw from
Burma, surely they'd have acted already? Megan wondered
if her cousin had gone back to the US. In her more paranoid
moments, early on, she'd convinced herself Luke was
involved in the kidnap.

But that was silly. The BMFF were passionate about their
cause. Luke wouldn't know a cause if it held a demonstration
on his street and tattooed a slogan on his forehead.

Something changed. It took Megan a moment to work
out what it was. Since she'd been moved to Burma, there'd
been a steady hum outside her door, like you got from a big

air conditioning unit, or an electricity generator.

The noise had stopped.

RANGOON, BURMA

The taxi driver didn't want to take Luke to the address, he wanted to take him to a hotel. But Luke wanted to get on with it. He had no time to waste. The promise of an extra twenty dollars soon changed the taxi driver's mind. The Chinatown side street was empty but for a wooden stall with striped plastic curtains. The driver pointed behind the stall.

'You want coke, hash, speed? I take you to better place.'

Ignoring him, Luke pushed the door open. It was dark.

'Syu?' No response. He felt around for a light switch. Nothing.

'Do you have a torch?' he asked the driver, who first shook his head, then produced a cigarette lighter.

The place was a mess. Rats scurried around. Behind a tatty screen, in a room on the left, were two fold-up chairs. There were cigarette butts and scraps of tin foil on the floor, an acrid, sour, chemical smell. A drugs den. Not a home. Luke sensed a trap. The text message, he decided, had been fake. It was designed to lure him here. But Ethan had got here first. So they had probably kidnapped him.

'Take me to a hotel,' he told the taxi driver. 'A good one.'

He had slept badly on the plane and worse the night before. There was nothing he could do at this time of night, except gather energy for tomorrow. Luke could think of three courses of action that he could follow, but was too tired to work out the consequences and likely chance of success of each.

'Strand Hotel, best place in Yangon,' the driver said.

'Fine,' Luke told him.

9.40 p.m. The city looked like it had closed down for the night. Luke hadn't visited Asia before and he wasn't interested in being a tourist this time. Rangoon might as well be a film set. For some weird reason, cars drove on the right, like at home, but the drivers sat on the right, like in the UK. It made it hard for them to see to overtake. His cab veered around a solitary coach. Luke noticed that the coach had exit doors on its left side, but they were taped over. This country would take time to understand.

The smart hotel they arrived at was straight out of some historical epic movie, just along the road from the British Embassy. His room cost less than a cheap room in a Manhattan dive. By the time he'd clambered beneath the mosquito net in his wide bed, he was too tired to call Flick, or Grace, or anybody else. He fell into a deep, long sleep.

Forty

ISLINGTON, LONDON

Luke didn't call. So much for his promise. It was midnight in Rangoon. Grace doubted that he'd phone tonight. Earlier, when she'd spoken to him, she'd forgotten to tell him that UK mobile phones didn't work in Burma. Which explained why she couldn't get through to Ethan but didn't explain how Megan had been able to send a text from there.

Grace had to do something. So far, she had avoided talking to Mum. Dad was away. Grace wasn't happy that the government hadn't intervened over Megan's kidnap. Even when they thought Megan was dead. Mum said Special Branch were keeping a close eye on the situation, but it was delicate. They couldn't encourage KI to give in to terrorists. Since the raid on the warehouse, Kite Industries had done nothing to help.

Grace feared that Ethan had run headlong into a trap. Now Luke was likely to do the same. She had to talk to someone, to do something. But she could only wait until he called her.

Grace put on the TV to distract herself. A soap opera that she liked was on, but she couldn't focus on the characters.

They were just actors reading out lines. Then she thought of something. Flick would be home by now. Luke hadn't taken her to Burma with him. But he was bound to have called her when he arrived, told her where he was staying. All Grace had to do was track down Flick.

What was her surname? Grace had no idea. Flick had only been Megan's personal assistant for a few weeks. She'd found her online. With luck, all of the details would be on Megan's laptop, which was still in the spare bedroom. Grace got the computer. It was password protected but Grace and Megan had been friends for a long, long time. She knew her passwords. Unless, that was, she had changed this one since she started going out with Grace's brother. No, Megan wasn't paranoid. Grace got into her email with no problem.

There were lots of saved emails from Ethan. Grace ignored those. Megan wasn't the most methodical of people. None of her emails were separated off into sub folders. It took a while, but she found what she was looking for: the initial email exchanges between Megan and Flick. They didn't give Flick's address, but there was a surname, Capaldi, and a mobile number. Grace rang it.

The call went straight to voicemail. Grace left a message, explaining why she needed to contact Luke urgently. 'Please call me as soon as you get this, whether you've heard from him or not. Day or night, please. I think he's in danger.'

She spent the rest of the evening waiting for her phone to ring.

RANGOON, BURMA

Luke woke with a clear head, no jet lag. He ordered breakfast in his room and thought through his options. Then he tried to call Flick on the hotel phone. The operator informed him that international lines were down and wouldn't be fixed until this evening.

'Does that happen often?' Luke asked.

'Quite often, yes.'

Luke had dual citizenship, but, given Ethan's nationality, it made sense to go to the British rather than the US Embassy. Megan's boyfriend might have gone to his country's embassy for advice. Luke checked his phone. He had a fairly good picture of Ethan and Megan together, taken just before she was kidnapped. If the embassy couldn't or wouldn't help, Luke had another option, but it wasn't one he was sure about taking.

The British Embassy was a large white building like ones he'd seen in Mayfair and smart parts of London. A row of trees lined its frontage. They were tidily trimmed, unlike the dark, scrubby trees that dominated many of Rangoon's streets.

Outside the canopied entrance, a balding man with black teeth and red lips called to him. 'Sir, you look to me like you require a guide. Can I be of assistance?'

Luke shook his head and went in to Reception. He explained who he was and asked to see the ambassador.

'How old are you?' The young male receptionist asked.

'Sixteen.'

'Are you with your parents? Perhaps—'

'Tell the ambassador that I'm Luke Kite. I'm the co-owner of Kite Industries, which has a large presence in Rangoon, and I'm here to deal with a serious, life-threatening problem that affects the son of a British government minister.'

The receptionist blinked, then excused himself. He returned a couple of minutes later with a thirty-something guy in a linen suit. The guy introduced himself as Robert Ward.

'The ambassador isn't in yet, but if you'd like to tell me your problem, I'll be in a position to brief him when he arrives.'

Luke did his best to explain what was going on. 'Are you aware of the kidnapping?' he finished.

'The ambassador has been made aware of the situation, but this is the first we've heard that Megan Kite might be here. As for the government minister's son, I'll have flight manifests checked at once, make sure that he actually arrived. This isn't a safe place, you know, especially with elections about to be announced. There have been several terrorist bombings. The government's doing its best to make sure they aren't reported. We've just changed the advice on the embassy website to tell potential tourists that it's too dangerous to travel here.'

'I'm pretty sure Ethan made it,' Luke said. 'It could be that they're holding him with Megan.'

'I'll also get somebody to check round all the hotels. He must have booked in somewhere. What do Kite Industries say?'

'Er . . .' Luke didn't want to explain that he didn't trust anybody at Kite Industries. 'I haven't been there yet. I thought it was important to talk to you guys first, Robert.'

'Call me Rob. I'm glad you came. Your company has better contacts in Rangoon than we do. It's much closer to the ruling regime. We aren't terribly popular with the junta.'

'I'm not sure how seriously they'll take me,' Luke admitted. 'I co-own the company, but that isn't widely known.'

'With Ms Kite missing, surely you're the most important person in the company structure.'

'How big is the KI operation in Burma?' Luke asked.

'Don't know. KI is very secretive. They operate not as KI, but as Myanmar Industrial. All we know is that they're supplying information technology to the Burmese government. Our assumption is that much of it is for surveillance purposes.'

'OK,' Luke said. 'If you think it's necessary, I'll go to the Myanmar Industrial offices, see what I can find out.'

'I'll have a car take you,' Rob told him.

'Thanks. Do you have a phone connection? I'm supposed to call Grace Thompson in the UK, tell her what's going on.'

'The phone lines are down, but I can sort you out with a satellite phone if it's urgent.'

'It is,' Luke said. 'She'll be worried sick.'

'Will she be awake? It's two in the morning there.'

Luke compromised by sending a text. On the way to his car at the back of the embassy compound, Rob took a call on his mobile, which was on the Burmese network.

'We've got confirmation from the flight manifest,' he told

Luke. 'Ethan Thompson did arrive in Rangoon two days ago. He hasn't left.'

Forty-One

MYANMAR INDUSTRIAL OFFICES, RANGOON

The manager of KI's Burmese operation was a tall, thirty-something American with a square jaw and blond hair that he kept close cropped. Josh Smith wore a beige, lightweight suit and Converse sneakers. He knew who Luke was, he said.

'I heard through the grapevine that your father's really Mike Kite, is that right?'

Luke nodded brusquely. 'What you won't have heard is that Megan Kite signed over half the company to me.'

'I hadn't heard that.' Smith gave no sign that he knew about Megan's kidnap, so Luke decided not to mention it.

'Check it out with Stella Lock if you like,' Luke said. He didn't want Stella talking to Josh, but it was the middle of the night in the UK, so there was no risk of that happening soon.

'Not necessary. I only have to look at you to know that you're your father's son. What brings you here?'

'Megan and I are interested in the Burmese operation.'

'We tend to refer to the country as Myanmar.'

'Sorry, that's what the generals like, isn't it? I want us to stay copacetic with the regime. These Eastern economies are our company's future. Why don't you show me around?'

'It'd be an absolute pleasure.'

Smith took Luke on a tour of the three-floor plant. Each floor consisted of rows of tables where programmers sat at computer terminals. Most of the workers appeared to be Burmese. As far as Luke could tell, they were operating on computers that were two or three years old.

'What sort of projects are you working on?' Luke asked.

'Software development,' Smith replied, cagily.

'Surveillance systems?'

'All kinds of monitoring, yes. This is a very closed society and before they open up the country technologically, the government wants to be sure they can keep a lid on things. Sudden change can be very disruptive.'

Luke tried to think what his Uncle Mike would say in this situation. 'Not our job to be moral arbiters,' he told Smith. 'We're here to make money.'

'Exactamondo! There are dozens of British companies making money here, from Lloyds of London to Rolls Royce.'

'And even more US ones, I expect.'

'More than I can count. Hey, you're your father's son! I worked with Mike over in North Korea for a while. He's quite a guy. I hope his present difficulties soon resolve themselves.'

'Was Mike involved in setting up the KI operation here?'

'Before my time. I think it was Jack.'

Luke scrunched up one of his eyebrows, consciously using another Mike gesture. It seemed that what Mike had told him at the Clinton Correction facility was true: his real father was responsible for starting KI's Burma operation.

The area they approached was protected by an ID card scanner at a manned security desk.

'What's behind those screens?' Luke asked

'That operation's on a need-to-know basis,' Josh apologized.

'I'm glad that you're keeping security tight,' Luke said, thinking about what his uncle would do in these circumstances. 'But I want to see the full story. Show me.'

Josh hesitated, but only for a moment. 'Of course, Mr Kite. But I should warn you, we have a very important visitor.'

'You mean *another* very important visitor,' Luke quipped.

Jake gave him a nervous smile. 'Come through,' he said, nodding at the Burmese man behind the security desk.

Two soldiers, armed with rifles, stood aside to let them pass. The area they entered was cooler than the previous zone, but equally dominated by computers. Only these computers weren't PCs, they were large white tablets on grey stands. Luke couldn't understand the writing on the tablet screens, but knew at once what the tablets were for. He'd seen them in US news stories, but wasn't old enough to use one yet. Voting machines.

'We're supplying the technology for the people of Myanmar to vote electronically?' he asked.

'Not quite,' Josh told him. 'The government has bought up a huge quantity of American voting machines. We're providing the software to make sure that the machines work efficiently.'

'There's somebody I'd like you to meet,' Josh said.

A frowning Burmese man emerged from behind one of the machines. He was paunchy, smaller than Luke and wore a sand-coloured military uniform festooned with medals.

'General Thieu!' Josh greeted him. 'I'd like to introduce Luke Kite, the heir to our great company, who has taken a particular interest in our work for you.'

The general's stern expression relaxed.

'I knew your father. A great man.'

Which father did he mean? Best not to ask.

'Thank you. I'm pleased that the company is able to continue Dad's work.'

'It would not be possible to hold these elections without Kite Industries' help. We are about to make a great announcement that will mark the next stage in Myanmar's transformation.'

'Great!' Luke said. 'Glad we're part of all this.'

'How long do you plan to stay in our country? There will be a dinner at the palace tomorrow to launch the election campaign. You must be a guest of honour!'

'That's very . . . generous of you,' Luke said, although he was aware of Josh giving the smallest shake of the head.

The general broke into a broad smile and offered Luke his hand. For such a slight man, he had a very firm handshake. Then he began to ask Josh questions. Luke stood back but listened carefully. What he heard wasn't surprising. Mike had hinted at the situation. It was shocking nevertheless. No wonder KI had been keeping its involvement in Burma secret.

BURMA

Ethan was tied to a hard chair, with his hands bound behind his back. They hadn't moved him at night, so he'd had to sleep in the chair too. The room had barely cooled off at all. He was sweating like a man who'd run a marathon. It wasn't just the heat. He kept thinking about Megan, how he'd drunkenly betrayed her by spending the night with Panya. Would she forgive him when she found out?

That night, he'd thought she was dead. He was devastated. Nothing he did seemed to matter. Panya was only trying to comfort him. But he wasn't sure Megan would see it that way. Megan liked black and white, not grey.

'Where's Megan?' Ethan asked, when the guy came to feed him. 'If you're going to kidnap me, the least you could do is put me with Megan.'

'Megan Kite is not here,' the young Burmese man said.

'Then where is she?'

'I don't know. Our organization works on a cell basis. If any of my group are caught, we cannot reveal anything significant about the rest of the organization.'

He left the room. In the corner of the room, Ethan spotted a large brown stain, the colour of dried blood. He prayed that it wasn't Megan's.

His captor returned.

'Your mother is a government minister.'

'That's right.'

'I think it's time that we contacted her,' the kidnapper calmly announced. 'Give me her telephone number.'

MYANMAR INDUSTRIAL
OFFICES, RANGOON

'Now I know why the government keeps postponing the election announcement,' Luke said, back in Josh Smith's office.

'It's not our fault. The generals keep changing the specifications for the voting machines. They want the right result, but it's also got to look convincing.'

Josh showed no shame that KI were fixing the election for the military dictatorship, so Luke played along.

'They want the international observers to report that everything was done fairly.'

'After which, the regime will come under less external pressure. They might even get aid from the First World again. We're on a hefty bonus if it all works out, as you'd expect.'

'You're doing an outstanding job, Josh. I'm impressed!' Luke slapped his back. 'When will the project be complete?'

'We're still tweaking the software upgrade that will give them everything they need. Running final tests today and delivering tomorrow, just before they announce the elections.'

'Before the dinner the general invited me to?'

'Yes. I did try to warn you against accepting the dinner invitation. It might not be wise to attend. We've kept Kite Industries involvement in Myanmar very quiet. Myanmar Industrial can be connected with Kite, but most of the real work we do is billed to a sham subsidiary company, Island Industrial.'

229

'I'd've thought the regime wants the election machinery to be associated with a major software firm like KI. That way, the world would be convinced that the election was honest.'

Luke stared at Smith, but the manager averted his eyes. Luke understood. KI wanted the vote-rigging work, but not the reputation that came with it. Luke broke into a smile.

'If the hands-off principle has been agreed with London and New York, then obviously I'll play along.'

Josh returned the smile, relieved not to have to contradict the young boss. 'I'm glad you see it that way, Luke. If they issue a formal invitation, I'll make a diplomatic excuse for you.'

'Just one thing. I want you to check with me before giving the regime the software upgrade. I might need to ask for a favour, see if the Burmese can find a missing friend of mine.'

'And you want some leverage? No problem. I tell you, these guys are eating out of our hands. We're going to make them respectable.'

ISLINGTON, LONDON

'I've spoken to Special Branch,' Mum told Grace at breakfast. 'If Megan's alive, she can't be in Burma. There wasn't enough time for her to be smuggled there.'

'Maybe the BMFF flew her there,' Grace argued.

'All air traffic is incredibly tightly controlled.'

'So you're giving up on her,' Grace complained.

'No. But this is a very sensitive time for the Burmese

government. They're about to invite official observers from the UN and elsewhere. I've let the Prime Minister know that I'm willing to go on behalf of the British government. If, by any chance, Megan really is there—'

Grace interrupted. 'Mum, the elections haven't been called yet. They must be weeks away! And the BMFF are bound to show the video that Megan made. Once they see that, the Burmese government won't be keen to help her.'

'Do you have a better idea?'

'Not exactly.' Grace tried to decide what to say. Overnight, Luke Kite had texted her to say that Ethan had probably been kidnapped. Luke thought she ought to tell Mum and Dad. She didn't like to do what Luke told her to, but had no choice. 'There's something I need to share with you.'

'What?'

'Ethan flew to Rangoon three days ago, to look for Megan. I haven't heard from him since.'

Forty-Two

Megan kept thinking about her mother and father. If there was an afterlife, she could be joining them both soon. How long had it been since the last visit from one of her captors? Days. It made her feel foolish, but Megan tried the door all the same.

Still locked. She banged on it. The act felt hopeless. What if her captors had fled, or been killed, leaving her to starve to death, alone? Megan was very hungry. She tried to focus on good things. She tried to remind herself what a lucky life she had had. How privileged she was compared to most of the world's people. Lots of them lost their parents young, and had crippling illness and poverty to contend with. All those terrible stories in the Burma videos they'd made her watch. If Megan got out of this, she would cherish her freedom. She'd use her money for good. She'd devote her life to helping others.

The noise outside the cell hadn't started up again, and the air was cold. Megan was beginning to doubt that she was in Burma. Surely Asian countries didn't get as cold as this? The kidnappers had left her a grubby, green sweater that she'd been using as a second pillow. She began to wear it.

How long had she been a captive? Hard to be sure, when

her days were so broken that she never got a full night's sleep. Two weeks, at least. Her stomach growled loudly. Megan never worried about her weight. When she came out of this she'd be waif thin. If she came out of this.

Megan picked up her water bottle. Barely 100 ml left. You couldn't live for long without water. Only a couple of days, she thought. How many times could you drink your own pee before it poisoned you: was it one or two? She may be about to find out.

ISLINGTON, LONDON

This time, the BMFF didn't put a brick through the window, but made a late-night phone call to the rarely used landline. Grace answered it.

'Florence Thompson please.'

'She's still at the Commons. This is her daughter, Grace.'

'This is the BMFF. We are holding your brother. In Rangoon. If you want to see him or his girlfriend again, your government will persuade Kite Industries to close its office in Burma and withdraw from the country with immediate effect. By "immediate", we mean tomorrow. No later. Understand?'

'What gives you the impression that my mum has that kind of power? She's only a—'

'That's your problem. KI must close down its office by the end of the working day tomorrow. We have been very patient but there arc many, many lives at stake. Including Ethan's and Megan's. Goodbye.'

Shaking, Grace called Mum and left a message on her machine. Then she called her dad but couldn't get through to him either. What was the name of that Special Branch guy? She had his number somewhere. Then she tried Luke. But, of course, his mobile didn't work in Burma.

Megan. Now Ethan. Was she fated to lose everyone she loved? Grace didn't know what to do. Her mobile rang. A number she didn't recognize.

'Grace? It's Luke Kite, calling from the British Embassy in Burma. I haven't tracked down Ethan yet, but I'm working on it. Have there been any developments at your end?'

Grace told him.

RANGOON, BURMA

Luke and Rob Ward had been at the embassy since dawn. They studied surveillance videos of the embassy's frontage from the previous three days.

'We found two possible sightings of Ethan Thompson,' Rob said. 'Here, at night.'

Footage of a tall, slim young man in a baseball cap peering under the canopy of the embassy entrance.

'Yeah, that could definitely be him.'

'And here, from the following morning, just before we opened.'

The daylight shot was much clearer.

'That's definitely him. Who's he talking to?'

'Not sure.'

Luke stared at the screen. 'I recognize that guy. He offered to be my guide.'

They watched Ethan leave with the Burmese man.

'We'd better locate him as soon as we can,' Rob said.

'Yesterday morning, he was standing outside when I arrived.'

Just before eight, the Burmese guy who had offered to be Luke's guide showed up at the embassy. He called himself Khin and spoke better English than half the kids Luke went to high school with. Khin explained how he had taken Ethan to the same address in Chinatown that Luke had visited.

'I sat beneath a tree at the edge of Resistance Park, waiting for him to return. But he did not. After half an hour, I walked over to the building he had visited, even though it looked like a drugs den.'

'And?' Rob asked.

'That is all. I asked the vendor at the stall in front of the building. She said two men had come out, carrying a heavy bundle, ten minutes before.'

'Did you hear anybody use the name *Syu*?' Luke asked.

Khin shook his head. His story didn't quite add up, Luke decided. Khin wouldn't go into the building with Ethan but then he went on his own. He said he was watching the building, but somehow didn't see the two men leaving with a bundle. He was lying about something, Luke figured. But he had more urgent things to deal with.

'I need to get hold of Stella Lock, the Kite Industries CEO, in London,' Luke told Rob. 'Can you do that?'

'Sure. But what are you going to ask her to do?'

'The thing the BMFF have been asking for all along: KI's complete withdrawal from Burma.'

'And what makes you think she'll agree?'

'I'll find a way to make her agree,' Luke said.

Stella Lock would be tough to negotiate with. She held all the cards. However Luke had two things going for him. With Ethan taken, the British government was bound to put pressure on KI to withdraw from Burma. Also, Luke knew about Island Industrial. His Uncle Mike had mentioned the sham company, then Josh Smith had confirmed its existence. Luke could offer Stella a compromise. Remove the main KI operation, but leave KI to finish the election job for the junta. That was the main thing the military government cared about.

Would the BMFF accept the closure of the KI plant and release Ethan and Megan? Luke didn't know. Closing down the vote-rigging operation was unnecessary, because the BMFF couldn't know about it. Also, it was too much to ask. From what Josh had told him, KI stood to lose billions if they failed to deliver on the election software. What the company was doing was wrong, Luke knew that. But he wasn't responsible. Friends and family came before politics. The Burmese people would have to lump it. Their government would always find a way to screw them, with or without KI's help.

His call came through.

'Luke, I'm so pleased to track you down,' Stella Lock said. 'I was beginning to think that you were avoiding me.'

Forty-Three

DOWNING STREET, LONDON

'You're getting this information from where?' the Prime Minister asked Florence Thompson. 'Your daughter?'

'Grace has talked to Luke Kite in Rangoon, where Ethan's being held. I'm sorry to burden you with this, Prime Minister. I'm at my wits' end.'

The PM said a few calming words, then thought aloud: 'Britain's biggest software company is setting up fraudulent voting machines. It's a joke. No matter how convincing the Burmese make the voting system, nobody will take the results seriously. Not when when the latest constitution guarantees that the army stays in power. Jack Kite knew that. He had no time for regimes like Burma's, but he wasn't averse to taking their money.'

The Prime Minister used to play golf with Jack Kite, Florence remembered. 'They're saying we have until the end of the working day tomorrow,' she reminded her boss.

'The Foreign Office say the election announcement is about to be made. We'd better act sooner rather than later. Without publicity, or we'll put more politician's children at risk. We'll get Ethan out, Florence. According to Special

Branch, the BMFF are ineffectual. They haven't hurt anybody so far.' The PM picked up his phone. 'I'd like you to put me through to Stella Lock at Kite Industries, please.'

'How can you be sure that she'll do what you want?' Florence asked, while the PM waited to be put through.

'Because I'm not going to offer her a carrot. I'm going to go straight in with a bloody big stick.'

The PM listened for a moment, then shouted, 'I don't care who she's in conference with. Tell her that, if I don't get her in the next minute, she can forget about the ID Card contract!'

'You're giving KI the contract for the national Identity Card database?' Florence asked.

'The contract hasn't been signed yet, but KI have spent years doing the groundwork. They're the best at what they do,' the PM said, then added, 'Why do you think the Burmese government were so keen to work with them?'

RANGOON, BURMA

'I hear what you're saying,' Stella told Luke. 'And, naturally, I want to oblige you. But it would mean breaking contracts.'

'That's been your position all along,' Luke said. 'And I'm telling you, you've got to shift your position, or the publicity will destroy the company. Think about it. Two deaths. Propping up a military junta. Don't make me threaten to give a press conference. I'd much prefer a compromise.'

'It's a tempting compromise,' Stella admitted. 'When I took over, I wasn't at all happy to find the company in this position. But do you really think we can leave the operation to complete and the BMFF will still release Ethan and Megan?'

'As long as the junta delay the election announcement until they're free, yes.'

'I'm not sure the BMFF are that stupid,' Stella said. 'Will you hold on, please? I have to take a very important call.'

What could be more important than this? Luke didn't know, but it was too late. She was gone. He sat by the embassy phone, waiting. Rob Ward joined him.

'If you can persuade KI to leave, we've reserved a plane that can take home all of the overseas nationals tonight.'

'That's great,' Luke said. 'But I'm not sure she's going to buy the deal. It's still giving in to blackmail.'

'Institutions give in to blackmail all the time,' Rob said. 'The key thing is that they aren't publicly seen to do so. The PM's office have been on to us in the last few minutes. I think things are starting to happen.'

Luke swore. 'If the UK government gets involved, that could screw the whole thing up. They won't want us to bargain with the BMFF.'

'Ethan Thompson's presence in Burma changes things. You might be pleasantly surprised.'

Stella Lock came back on the line.

'The compromise you suggested was an astute one, Luke. You've clearly got your father's head for business. But if we're going to pull out, we can't take risks with Megan and Ethan's lives. I've decided to close down the complete KI operation in Burma, including the Island Industrial department, with immediate effect. I need to ensure that we can get our people out safely. Is anybody from the embassy with you?'

Luke handed the phone over to Rob Ward, who told Stella about the plane they had lined up.

'Result!' Rob said, when he was finished on the phone. 'Stella Kite is going to talk to Josh Smith straight away.'

'He won't be happy,' Luke said.

'Not our problem. Our problem is finding Ethan Thompson and Megan Kite.'

'I don't think Megan's in Burma,' Luke said. 'We need to get Ethan home before the junta get wind of what we're up to.'

'I can't see how we can expedite his release so quickly.'

'I have an idea how we might find him,' Luke said. 'Is Khin still hanging around outside? I think he might be willing to act as our guide.'

Forty-Four

They came for him in the middle of the afternoon, when the day was at its hottest. Ethan had no idea what to expect. With the guard was a visitor who Ethan recognized. The middle-aged man spat in the corner before speaking. Ethan realized that what he'd thought was dried blood was spit full of betel juice. Megan could still be alive. Would they take him to her? And if they did, should he tell her about Panya? Sometimes, his politician parents said, lies were kinder than the truth.

'Hello, Ethan.'

'Khin? Were you always part of this?'

'I'm afraid so,' his former guide said. 'I'm sorry that it was necessary for me to deceive you, but my motives were pure, I assure you. And now I am returning you to your friends.'

'Which friends?'

'A young man called Luke Kite found me earlier. He was not as convinced by my performance as a guide as you were. He asked me to organize your release. He has expedited KI's withdrawal from Burma, as the Democracy movement have requested. He only asks that I get you to the airport in time to join the departing workers.'

Was it a bluff? Ethan couldn't believe that, after

stonewalling for so long, KI would give in so easily.

'You look suspicious,' Khin said, 'but we have spies at KI's Rangoon office. Everything is being closed down in great secrecy, including their secret operation to manipulate our elections. We will keep our side of the bargain.'

'What about Megan? Will she be freed too?'

'Of course.'

'Will she be on the plane with me?'

'No. She has never been in Burma.'

'Then where is she?'

'I'm afraid that we work in a cell structure. We are only—'

'Told what you need to be told so you can't give anything away,' Ethan finished for him. 'I've heard that speech before.'

'I'm afraid I'm going to have to put you in the boot of a taxi to get you to the airport,' Khin said. 'We will take back roads, for the army is on high alert. We must leave at once.'

RANGOON

Josh Smith gave a face-saving speech about the money they were throwing away, then agreed to do what his boss said. Even so, Rob Ward stuck with Josh all the time, making sure he didn't double-cross them by telling the junta the plan. Luke thought that the embassy man was being over cautious. Josh wouldn't disobey orders from Stella Lock. If Josh tried to help out the Burmese and stayed to organize the electoral fraud, the American would be stuck in Rangoon for good. In the business world beyond, he would be dead meat. No amount of cash was worth a lifetime trapped in backward, totalitarian Burma.

Rob answered the phone, spoke a few words of Burmese, then turned to Luke.

'Khin has confirmed that he was able to collect Ethan, and they're on the way to the airport. The plane's refuelling as we speak. It's time to go.'

Rob had organized three minibuses and two limousines, providing enough seats to ferry everybody to the airport. The Burmese nationals who had been working on the election project were still in the office, running unnecessary tests on the voting machines. They could not be trusted to know what was going on. Some were bound to inform the junta. In Burma, Rob said, there were secret agents all over, spying for the government in every part of society, at every level.

'Will the generals be able to fix the election with what they've learned from you?' Luke asked Josh.

'Not unless they keep out international observers then lie about the results,' Josh said. 'As things stand, they're well placed to run an honest, efficient election with modern voting machines. I'm sure the junta will love that.'

Luke smiled. Josh still thought that Luke was on his side. He knew that Luke had suggested letting the electoral fraud go ahead but been overruled.

'Uh-oh,' the American said. 'I think those guys are coming for you.'

Two Burmese soldiers were in the KI lobby. They watched office workers carry heavy bags and boxes out to the vehicles.

'For me?' Luke said. This was about to go horribly wrong.

'Can I help you?' he asked the soldiers, but they didn't appear to speak English.

'Luke Kite?' said the taller of the two soldiers, pointing at Luke.

'Yes.' Stupid to deny it.

'General Thieu requests your company!' The smaller one grasped his arm.

'Why?' Was he being arrested? Luke didn't know what to do. Josh waved at Rob Ward, but the embassy official had faded into the background when he saw the soldiers. His presence might give the game away.

Luke had an idea.

'We need a translator here!' he shouted, waving at Rob. 'You're the KI translator, aren't you?'

Rob hurried over, adopting the part. 'What's going on?'

'These guys want to take me somewhere,' Luke told him.

Rob began to speak in rapid Burmese. At first, he was smiling. Then his face became tense.

'They're taking you to the palace for dinner with the dictator. Why would that be?'

'I met the general yesterday,' Luke remembered. 'He wanted me to go to the palace for a dinner to celebrate the election announcement.'

'I think there was a formal invitation,' Josh said. 'I'm afraid I've been too preoccupied to find a way to decline it.'

Luke's spirits sank. Was this some kind of revenge on Josh's part? The KI boss avoided looking in Luke's direction.

'I guess you have to go,' Rob said.

'But our flight leaves in less than two hours!'

'Hush!' Rob said. 'Those two are bound to know some words of English.' He smiled at the soldiers, then spoke in Burmese. The soldiers listened carefully and nodded.

'What did you tell them?' Luke asked.

'That you needed to change and would be ready in a few minutes. We have to get out of here *now*. This could mess up everything.'

The soldiers remained at the front doors of the offices, waiting to escort Luke.

'What's the official explanation for our flight?' Luke asked Rob.

'It's a private plane for KI operatives whose contract has finished. But that story won't hold up if any of the Burmese workers we've left behind get in touch with intelligence here.'

'Which could happen any time,' Josh pointed out.

The soldiers were talking. One checked his watch, then spoke to Rob, who translated.

'He says they can take you to your hotel for clothes, but you must leave now.'

'All my clothes are packed,' Luke said. 'I'd better go with him now, or I could screw everything up for Ethan and Megan.'

'You could end up being trapped here,' Rob warned.

'You'll still be here won't you? I'm a friend of the regime. I'll be OK. Get out now. This way, at least Ethan and Megan will be safe. I can look after myself.'

Rob gave him a look that said, *But you're only sixteen*. Then he did as Luke asked and told the soldiers to take him to the dinner.

On the street outside, huge crows swooped to raid food from open bins. Luke ducked to avoid one of them. He had never felt so alone.

AIRPORT ROAD, RANGOON

'This is where we are meant to meet your friend,' Khin said.

The Burmese man helped Ethan to get out of the car's boot. He had been there for ages and was stiff. It was evening. They were at the end of a side road that adjoined the main road to the airport. Khin looked anxious. Army patrols came down this road, Ethan remembered from his arrival in Burma.

This would be his last contact with the kidnappers. There were questions he needed to ask.

'Has Megan been released? he asked.

'I expect so. We are people of our word. We would not have taken these actions if there were any choice.'

This answer irritated Ethan. 'Do you really think your Democracy movement leaders would sanction kidnapping?'

'Sometimes, it is better for leaders not to know everything that is done in their name.'

'Do you know how angry that makes me?' Ethan asked.

Khin gave him a thin smile. 'We have a saying: "To be angry is to revenge the faults of others on ourselves".'

'Spare me the proverbs,' Ethan said. 'You don't really think that KI withdrawing from Burma will have any lasting effect on the regime, do you?'

'We are in a long war. It is a small victory. The first

victory we have had for a while,' Khin said. 'One never knows how significant a battle is until the war is over. Here are your friends.'

A convoy of limousines and minibuses was coming down the road. The first long, black limousine pulled over at the junction. A thirty-something guy in long khaki shorts hurried over to Ethan and Khin.

'Ethan Thompson? I'm Rob Ward from the British Embassy. Have they given you back your passport?'

Khin handed the passport to Ethan. 'Please apologize to your family and friend for the inconvenience we have put them to.'

Ethan nodded brusquely. Rob pointed to the limousine.

'Where's Luke?' Ethan asked him.

'Never mind that now. Let's get the hell out of here.'

IMPERIAL PALACE, RANGOON

The generals had Burmese clothes waiting for him. Luke changed into a lilac top, like that worn by most of the civilian men at the dinner, and a purple *longyi*. It looked stupid, but was pretty comfortable in the humidity.

The huge dining hall was awash with flowers. The centrepiece of the decorations was a gigantic carved brown elephant with a red cape, draped with flowers. Its tusks were real ivory.

Luke was given a place of honour, to the left of General Thieu, only three places away from the dictator, beneath a crystal chandelier. Before sitting down, Luke was introduced to the Chairman of the Council, Head of State, Secretary of Defence and Commander-in-Chief of the armed forces. They were all the same person, a shrunken man with tired eyes. The dictator spoke to Luke and his translator interpreted.

'The chairman is looking forward to retirement. He will be able to do this – after the elections which your company has been so helpful with.'

Luke tried to think of something to say in return. He remembered a slogan he'd seen on a poster in his hotel.

'Kite Industries are honoured and glad to support Myanmar's Road Map to Democracy,' he told the dictator.

This went down well. The junta members were being so warm to him that Luke had to remind himself – these were dangerous, corrupt people. According to Rob Ward, most of the government's wealth came from drugs. Burma supplied all of the heroin in the US and the UK, producing sixty per cent of the world's total. No wonder the government could afford to pay KI so well.

The dinner guests sat on a long table facing out on to the ballroom. The remaining tables were arranged in vertical rows in front of them, with the guests on two-seater sofas. There was a toast. Luke raised his glass, though he couldn't understand a word that was being said. Two hundred people stood and chanted the words.

Somebody tapped Luke's shoulder. He jumped. At any moment, word might come through that KI had deserted the country, leaving behind the voting machines but without the crucial election software. He turned. A slight Burmese man smiled at him.

'I am your translator, Cobar. Anything you would like to say, you only have to ask.'

Toast over, General Thieu turned to Luke and asked, through the translator, when Mike Kite would be released.

'We hope to welcome him to Myanmar soon.'

'So do I,' Luke said. 'But it's in the hands of the American authorities.'

'You are an American citizen, I believe.'

'Yes, my mother is American.'

'That is very useful.'

The conversation continued at this level of banality for some time. Luke refused wine from a gold-stemmed goblet, and sipped soup. He tried to resist looking at his watch. General Thieu asked him how close he was to his sister.

'I have seen photographs of her, a very beautiful young woman.'

Luke would hardly go that far, but nodded enthusiastically.

'We didn't see very much of each other growing up, but we're running KI together now, so I think we'll become close partners.'

'In time, I think, you will become the senior partner. For she is bound to wish to get married and have children, yes?'

'We haven't discussed that,' Luke said.

The Burmese mobile phone in his shirt pocket began to ring. There were shocked glances from the tables facing them. You didn't carry a mobile phone when having dinner with the dictator. Luke apologized profusely.

'I was asked to carry this in case of emergencies.'

The phone that Rob had given him kept ringing. Everyone in the hall was staring at Luke like he'd dropped his pants. Luke took the phone out of his pocket. He didn't turn it off. He didn't answer it either, but looked to his right. The Head of State said something and General Thieu gave him a tight smile.

'Please,' he said through the translator. 'Answer your call.'

Luke pressed *receive*.

'They're all through Immigration,' Rob Ward told him. 'How do you want to proceed?'

Luke hesitated. He hadn't expected to have a translator so nearby when he took this call. He had to improvise and hope that Rob would work out how to play along.

'My sister's been kidnapped?' he said. 'That's terrible!'

He turned to General Thieu and began to babble.

'Something awful has happened at home. My sister Megan has been taken by kidnappers. We don't know who they are or what they want. And I'm so far away.'

As the translator explained what Luke had said, Luke began to speak to Rob in theatrically loud tones.

'I have to get home at once. When's the next plane to the UK? Please find out. I'll hold the line.'

Through the translator, General Thieu began to ask Luke questions. Luke worried that he'd gone too far. None of the two hundred guests were sipping their soup any more. They were all watching him. If his performance failed to convince, he was inflicting a huge insult on the generals, one they were bound to make him pay for. He covered his ear, pretending to be taking in complicated news.

'I see,' he said. 'I don't know. Is there someone there who speaks Burmese? Perhaps you could speak to General Thieu?'

He handed the phone to the army officer, knowing that his fate was in the general's hands.

MINGALADON INTERNATIONAL AIRPORT, RANGOON

Rob Ward ushered the group through to the Departures area. He checked his watch.

'The plane's ready to leave. There's no reason why the Burmese should block your exit. But I'll stay here until I'm sure the plane's gone, to be on the safe side.'

'Can't you come with us?' Ethan asked. 'I feel terrible, leaving you and Luke behind.'

'Luke's situation is in hand. And my job is here.'

'Won't there be repercussions when KI fail to fix the election?'

Rob shook his head. 'You don't understand Burma. The authorities will not admit that anything untoward has happened. Life will go on. Once the Burmese KI programmers realise they've been left out in the cold, there'll be a firestorm, but not in public. The junta may delay the election announcement. That's all.'

From the street outside came the sound of sirens. Ethan looked across the atrium. A military convoy.

'They've sussed us!' he said. 'They're going to stop us leaving.'

'It'll be all right,' Rob told him. 'I'll go down and greet them. Get on the plane.'

But Ethan couldn't go. He needed to see what happened. On the plane, he would be trapped, powerless. He had been locked up for three days. If they were going to keep him here, he would rather be out in the open, for a while at least.

A jeep mounted the pavement outside the airport entrance. Two soldiers jumped out. Between them was a woman in purple. They crashed through the doors and Ethan saw that it wasn't a woman, but a boy in a skirt. His girlfriend's brother.

'Get on the plane,' Rob told Ethan. 'I'll sort this out.'

Five minutes later, Ethan was sat at the front of the 747, in First Class. The other passengers had boarded before him and were getting restless.

'Why are we waiting?' a square-jawed American asked. 'Have we been found out? Are they going to haul us back to Rangoon?'

Then the door opened for a final time. Luke Kite hurried down the aisle, his skirt catching on the seatbelt when he sat down next to Ethan.

'Are we OK to go?' Ethan asked.

'Any minute. Once we're in the air, we're OK. The generals think I've hitched a ride on a private flight to deal with a sudden emergency. But all it takes is one phone call or for them to smell a rat, and we could be stuck here.'

The plane began to taxi. Nobody spoke. Luke kept taking deep breaths. Ethan realized that he was doing the same. The plane picked up speed. The pilot, it seemed, was in as much of a hurry to take off as the passengers. There was the usual deep, ominous rattle and rumble. Then they were

252

airbound. Everyone on the plane broke into applause. People cheered. Drinks appeared. Ethan felt himself begin to relax.

'I can't begin to thank you enough . . .' he told Luke.

'Don't sweat it,' Luke said. 'We both did what we had to do to help out Megan. Right now, there's only one thing on my mind. My stuff's all in the hold. Rob said you had hand luggage.'

'That's right.'

'We're about the same size, aren't we? I can't land in the UK looking like this. Can you lend me some clothes?'

Forty-Five

Megan was sleeping when she thought she heard a key in the lock outside. She jerked awake and called out. No noises. Not even retreating footsteps. She switched on the light in her cell. It was starting to fade. No food or drink had been brought in. Her mouth was ashtray dry. She had nothing left to drink or eat. Her body was running low on energy, but she banged on the door a few times in a token effort. Then, also a token effort, she tried the door handle. It turned, as it always did. She pushed, preparing to meet the resistance of a bolt or padlock.

And, this time, the door opened.

She stepped outside. There to her left, was a large, old-fashioned heating unit, which had been unplugged. That explained the noise that had stopped and why it was colder outside the cell than inside. There was a small power pack, which must have been what provided the electricity for her cell's forty-watt overhead light bulb. A padlock, left open, by the door. Nothing else. She crossed the room, looking warily at the floor, in case of holes in rotten floorboards. She got to a window and stared at the disused factory buildings that surrounded her. The room was high enough for her to see the grey, rainy landscape beyond. Definitely not Burma. London.

The building she was in resembled the one they'd held her in before. There was a central stairwell. She hurried down it as fast as her weak legs would take her. One side of the double door on the ground floor was open. A large rat ran across the concrete floor. Megan stepped out into a pale, drizzly autumn evening. She was in an industrial wasteland of some kind, surrounded by warehouse buildings with smashed windows and graffitied walls. Not far away, she could hear the steady rumble of traffic.

She began to walk towards the sound.

GATWICK AIRPORT, LONDON

Luke and Ethan parted in the Arrivals lounge. Ethan was going straight to the hospital where Megan was being treated for dehydration. Luke would like to go with him, but there was something he had to do first.

'Tell her I'll be there tomorrow to bring her home.'

'I will,' Ethan promised Luke. For somebody who was about to see the girlfriend who he'd thought was dead, Ethan looked surprisingly subdued, Luke thought. That was probably down to all the things he'd been through.

Luke felt like celebrating. They'd been through some stuff, but nobody had died, not even in the warehouse explosion. Ethan's ex-girlfriend had got that wrong.

Talking of girlfriends, Luke had something he needed to sort out.

'There's Flick,' Ethan said. 'I'll leave you two to reacquaint yourselves. Thanks for everything, Luke.'

Eef leaned forward as though to hug him. Luke gripped his hand instead. Then he hurried over to Flick. She was wearing blue jeans and a Shetland wool sweater, hardly her usual glamorous look. Luke preferred her this way. They kissed.

'I've missed you so much,' she said. 'I can't believe we haven't spoken since Aegina.'

'Let's talk about it in the car,' Luke told her.

'The Burmese government have delayed their elections. It was on the news this morning.'

'I heard,' Luke said. 'I'm glad some good has come out of this.'

Behind Luke, Kite employees were being hustled through for a debrief. Josh Smith wasn't among them. He had transferred to a flight for the US when they refuelled in Amsterdam. Josh wasn't happy with the kidnap's outcome. KI's software for the election had been deleted at the last minute, with the generals none the wiser until the British Airways plane was out of Burmese air space. Josh would not be welcome back in Burma while the regime remained in power. But he would bounce back, Luke thought. People like him always did.

'I'll bet you can't wait to get back to the Barbican,' Flick said, once they were in her car.

'I can't wait to see Megan,' Luke told her. 'We've got a lot of catching up to do. How have you been?'

'Worried about you, mainly. Burma's not a safe place.'

'Nobody tried to kidnap me,' Luke said. 'At least, not in Burma. But I've been thinking a lot about what happened in

Greece. Have you heard from Celine?'

'She hasn't returned my calls. I don't think she likes me very much. I don't know why.'

'Maybe she has the same doubts that I do,' Luke said.

'What do you mean?' Flick asked, glancing away from the road ahead so that she could see the expression on his face.

Luke chose his words carefully. 'There was something suspicious about how quickly the BMFF found us on Aegina.'

'It was a trap, surely, set up by that guy you met there?'

'I don't think so,' Luke said. 'I don't know how John Turner fits in with my dad's disappearance but I doubt he had anything to do with the kidnapping. I'm also trying to work out why the BMFF didn't hold you with me and Celine.'

'I'm not a member of the Kite family.' Flick's voice had become higher than it usually was. 'I wasn't any use to them when it came to putting pressure on KI.'

Luke ignored this point. 'While I was in Rangoon, I worked out some timelines. In Nice, the BMFF must have had notice that I was going to be there, because they sent two English guys over to try and take me. In Greece, I was surprised when the BMFF let Celine and me go . . .'

'I left you a note about that. They said they wanted to prove that they could get you whenever they wanted to.'

'I know that's what you said. But I worked out that they let us go just after they realized they'd captured a British government minister's son. They didn't need another hostage.'

'That makes sense.'

'What doesn't make sense was that, each time the BMFF tried to take me, in Nice and on Aegina, only two people knew where I was. You, and Celine.'

Flick slowed down the car.

'How long have you belonged to the BMFF?' Luke asked her.

Flick hesitated before replying. Her voice became deeper, older.

'Since I was fourteen. I was a founder member.'

'You were always using me to keep tabs on the investigation into the kidnapping.'

'It was like that at first,' Flick said. 'But I thought, when you found out what was going on, we'd be on the same side.'

'Which made it OK for you to set me up to be kidnapped?'

'I really do have feelings for you, Luke,' she said. He realized that he was hearing her real voice for the first time. More educated, more mature, almost condescending. 'Holding you and Celine to ransom made sense. It put pressure on KI to do the right thing.'

'Two wrongs can't make a right,' Luke argued.

'Why not? Nobody got hurt. The worse thing that happened was we had to leave Megan without water for a couple of days when we thought that KI were on to her new location. As soon as we heard that KI had caved in, I went over and unlocked her myself. Everything worked out the way we wanted it to. There's no betrayal here. I'm one of the good guys.'

'Everybody thinks they're one of the good guys,' Luke said. 'But I judge people by their actions. Lying, kidnapping

– those aren't the actions of good guys. They're what the villains do.'

'I wish you wouldn't be like this,' Flick argued.

'How old are you, really?'

'Twenty. I lied about my age because it was important that I be the same age as Megan to get the job with her. What happened between us was never part of a plan.'

'Megan could have died when KI raided that warehouse.'

'Millions of people have died in Burma because of the regime, Luke. Megan agreed with us in the end. You saw the video she made. The three of us did a good thing here.'

'Did we?' They had reached the Barbican. Flick got out the swipe card that allowed them access to the car park at the edge of the estate.

'I'll take that,' Luke said.

'What?'

'Let me out here. We're finished. If there's any of your stuff in the apartment, I'll have it sent on to you. That's if you're willing to give me your real address.'

'Don't be like this, Luke,' Flick pleaded, as he got out of the car.

'I really am like this,' Luke replied, a ton of resentment and disgust coming out in his voice. 'I've always been like this. I don't know what you're really like. And I don't want to find out.'

Forty-Six

THE BARBICAN, LONDON, THREE DAYS LATER

It was a crisp, clear October morning. Luke stood on the penthouse balcony and gazed at the city spread out beneath him, vaster than Manhattan. Could he get used to living here?

A cold wind picked up and he went back inside. Megan turned off the news.

'Nothing about the elections in Burma.'

'I can't believe how KI got an injunction to keep everything out of the newspapers,' Luke told her. 'When it comes to secrecy, the UK's almost as bad as Burma.'

'What's wrong with protecting our own?' Megan asked. 'Do you want KI to get a reputation for giving in to terrorists?'

'They weren't exactly terrorists, though, were they?'

'You mean they weren't ruthless enough?'

'Something like that.' Luke joined her on the sofa. Megan had been released from hospital two hours before, so this morning was their first chance to talk properly. He'd already told her the first of the two most important things.

'Have you heard from Flick?' Megan asked.

Luke shook his head. 'And I don't expect to.'

'I can't believe how she conned us both. I worked it out when I overheard a conversation about the BMFF having someone close to the investigation. When did you work it out?'

'For certain? Not until I was on the plane home.'

'Did you ever suspect I might be in on it?' Megan asked.

'After I saw that video you made, sure. But I figured that, if you knew about what Kite Industries was up to in Burma, you'd have played it straight. You'd have insisted that KI pull out, not go to ridiculous lengths like getting yourself kidnapped.'

'If the BMFF had come to me in the first place, I think I'd have helped,' Megan said. 'But I can't help them now, not even if I decided to. They've gone completely underground. I might give some money to *Free Burma Now!* instead. Do you think I should?'

'Whatever you want,' Luke said. 'But if you take out a membership, don't try to sign me up. I'm not much of a joiner.'

He got them both a soda.

'What's next?' he asked Megan. 'I figure we should arrange to see Celine. There's a lot I have to tell you about her.'

'OK. But I need a holiday first. You could come with me.'

'You and Ethan must need some time alone.'

'Maybe, but I don't want to leave you behind,' Megan said.

'Someone's got to keep an eye on what's happening at KI.'

'Look at Mr Responsible!'

Luke cringed.

'I'm so glad about the test result,' Megan said.

'It's funny,' Luke said, 'officially, we've always been brother and sister, but now loads of people think that Mike's my real dad. I don't know how to change that.'

'It doesn't matter. What matters is that we stay tight. I gave you half the company because I wanted to keep you close, no matter what our blood relationship was.'

'Now I'm your brother again, do you want me to give it back?' Luke asked.

Megan laughed. 'With everything you did in Burma, you've more than proved that I made the right decision.'

'Ethan tried to help,' Luke pointed out. 'If he hadn't taken a risk, got himself captured, you'd still be stuck in North London somewhere while I was being comforted by Flick.'

'Maybe so, but it was you who fixed things. You who made things happen. I couldn't be more proud of you.'

Luke felt his face redden. Should he be proud of himself? All he'd done was muddle through. He'd made a few decisions, more by instinct than intellect, and the results had worked out. He could take credit for the way things went right. That was what successful people did. But things were bound to go wrong, too. Would he be responsible for them as well?

'We got lucky,' he told Megan. 'We ought to learn from what happened and be more careful next time, more prepared.'

'You're right,' Megan said. 'And whatever happens next, we're in this together.'

'Always,' Luke agreed.

They fell into a long silence. Megan finished her drink.

'Do you think there's any chance that Dad's still alive?' Megan asked, at last.

Luke hesitated. He didn't want to raise Megan's hopes, or his own. He knew how much hung on what he said next.

'A ghost of a chance,' he said, finally.

A Note from the Author

I've visited all of the locations in this novel bar one. Most opposition groups in Burma are against tourism, for reasons made clear in the preceding pages. Therefore I did not visit Burma, but relied on written, video and online resources to help me portray the country. When it comes to the ruling junta's corrupt behaviour, I have only been able to scratch the surface.

If you're concerned about the situation in Burma, visit *www.burmacampaign.org.uk* for information. Please consider making a donation to them. The campaign groups mentioned in *Bad Company* are, I should add, entirely fictional.

Thanks to Allison, Emily, Laura, Lucy, Penny and Sue for their help with *Bad Company*. The Kite Identity series will continue with *Everybody Lies*.

Follow Harry on Twitter at https://twitter.com/kiteidentity

Read the first adventure:

Kite Identity Book One:

SOFT TARGETS
Harry Edge

Luke Kite has spent his life estranged from his father, multi-millionaire Jack Kite, and his half sister Megan.

But Jack's death and the sinister circumstances surrounding it mean that the Kite legacy is under threat.

Luke and Megan are drawn together in a partnership that will endure through a terrifying game of cat and mouse. From London, through New York to Tokyo; a dangerous web of lies and deceit unravels, and the Kite identity is revealed . . .